"You're insufferable."

Tamara glared at Kiel before she continued. "Get out before I scream."

"Would you really do that?" Kiel looked amused by her erratic behavior and walked over to where she sat.

"Yes, I would." She spat the words out.

"But there's no one to hear."

"We do have neighbors," she told him caustically.

"In that case, I shall have to stop you." His mouth was on hers almost before he finished speaking.

Tamara could not ignore the undisguised pleasure that ran through her. Even her anger and her hatred paled beside this much stronger emotion. When his kiss deepened, she kissed him back with breathless hunger.

"Proof, indeed, that I could make love to you anytime I wanted to," Kiel muttered against her lips.

Margaret Mayo began writing quite by chance when the engineering company she worked for wasn't very busy and she found herself with time on her hands. Today, with more than thirty romance novels to her credit, she admits that writing governs her life to a large extent. When she and her husband holiday—Cornwall is their favorite spot—Margaret always has a notebook and camera on hand and is constantly looking for fresh ideas. She lives in the countryside near Stafford, England.

Books by Margaret Mayo

AN IMPOSSIBLE SITUATION

Margaret Mayo

Harlequin Books

TORONTO • NEW YORK • LONDON
AMSTERDAM • PARIS • SYDNEY • HAMBURG
STOCKHOLM • ATHENS • TOKYO • MILAN
MADRID • WARSAW • BUDAPEST • AUCKLAND

Original hardcover edition published in 1990
by Mills & Boon Limited

ISBN 0-373-03190-4

Harlequin Romance first edition April 1992

AN IMPOSSIBLE SITUATION

CHAPTER ONE

THE unexpectedness of her beloved father's death had shocked Tamara deeply, but now to discover that he had left the firm to Kiel Kramer was more than she could comprehend. 'Why, Mummy? Why? Why has Daddy done this? He knew I always wanted to take over.'

Tamara Wilding was a younger version of her mother, a very beautiful girl with high cheekbones and brown, wide-spaced, sloe-shaped eyes, which at this moment were appealing and sad. Her fine brows were perfectly arched and her straight nose tilted up very slightly at the tip. Her lips were sensual, although fuller and less wide than she would have liked. She was slender with small, high breasts and carried herself proudly. Heads turned wherever she went, though invariably Tamara was unaware of it.

This morning she was wearing a short, black, stretch wool dress, the long sleeves and deep V neck embroidered in a bold tulip design with orange rayon. It clung to and accentuated her curves and she wore absolutely no jewellery. The effect was stunning. Her stockings too were sheer and black and her high-heeled shoes were of the very finest leather.

She sat on the settee next to her mother, one long leg elegantly crossed over the other. 'Mummy, can you give me some sort of an explanation? How could he do this to me? And to bring in Kiel Kramer of all people—I can't believe it.'

5

'Tammy, love.' Mrs Wilding stroked her daughter's enviable waist-length black hair back off her face. 'You're a brilliant designer, one of the best. Your father thought you'd be wasting your talents.'

'I could do both,' she protested.

'Ben didn't think so.'

'You knew I was never going to inherit, didn't you?' said Tamara resentfully. 'Daddy was humouring me. He hoped I'd change my mind. I wish you'd told me— I could have been prepared. I never expected anything like this. Never.'

'Your father did what he thought was best, Tamara, love,' said Mrs Wilding quietly, deeply unhappy by the way her daughter was taking the news. 'He did a lot of hard thinking before he made his decision.'

'I hate Kiel,' spat Tamara viciously, her brown eyes hard.

Mrs Wilding shook her head sadly. 'Once you've had time to come to terms with things you'll realise that it's all for the best.'

'Best for whom?' demanded Tamara. 'Not me, that's a fact. Has Kiel already taken over?' Tamara had been in Japan studying enamelling techniques when her father had died. She had come home for his funeral and then gone back to tie up loose ends before assuming control. And now she had returned to this! It was unbelievable.

Her mother nodded. 'Some weeks ago, in fact. He's fitted in very well. The staff like him, he's picked things up quickly, and your father had no qualms at all about leaving things in his capable hands.'

'But Daddy didn't know he was going to die—did he?' Suspicion tempered her last words. Was this something else that had been kept from her?

'He wasn't well,' said her mother, her mouth twisting wryly as she made the admission. 'His heart had been troubling him these last few months. He was thinking about retiring.'

Tamara almost exploded. 'And you didn't tell me?' It was unbelievable that they had kept their only daughter in ignorance of something as momentous as this.

'We didn't want to alarm you, love.' Hilary Wilding's tone was soothing as she stroked the back of Tamara's hand.

'But it was your intention all the time to ask Kiel to take over instead of me?' Tamara could not take in all she was hearing. She stood up abruptly. 'I'm sorry, Mummy, I can't sit and take this. I'm going to see Kiel. This thing has to be sorted out right now.'

'It wouldn't help, love, it's all legal.' Mrs Wilding stood too and looked as though she would have liked to forcibly restrain her daughter. 'Oh, dear, I didn't expect any of this.'

'And I didn't expect to hear that that man had taken the firm from under my very nose. If you think I'm going to sit back and let it happen, then you've another think coming.'

The older woman shook her head worriedly. 'There's not a thing you can do about it, Tammy. Why don't you at least wait until tomorrow, until you've had time to cool down? Arguing with Kiel won't get you anywhere.'

'I don't want to get anywhere with him, I just want to give him a piece of my mind.' Tamara stood tall and proud and beautiful, even more beautiful in her anger, her cheeks warmed with colour, her eyes shining. 'This is an impossible situation. How can I work for Kiel Kramer when we hate each other's guts?'

Mrs Wilding shook her head. 'I wish you didn't, I wish you got on. He's a fine man.'

'In your's and Daddy's eyes only. Excuse me, Mummy, I have to go. I won't sleep tonight if I don't sort this thing out.'

Her father's jewellery manufacturing company was in the famed Jewellery Quarter in Hockley, the other side of Birmingham from where they lived. Tamara backed her sporty Honda out of their three-car garage, and all the time she had this vision of a tough, uncompromising face, brown hair cut brutally short, and a mouth that was permanently grim.

The city traffic seemed more heavy than usual, or was it because she was in a hurry? Every traffic-light was on red, a lorry had shed its load forcing her to make a detour, and when she finally swung her car into the tiny car park at the rear of her father's premises Tamara was ready to start World War III.

It came as a bitter disappointment to discover that Kiel was out. 'He shouldn't be long,' said Carol, Ben Wilding's secretary of many years.

'Then I'll wait,' announced Tamara firmly.

'We really miss your father,' said Carol sympathetically. 'We were all very shocked when he died, but Mr Kramer is doing an excellent job in his place.' Carol was thirty-five and single and, judging by the expression on her face, had already fallen for the redoubtable Kiel Kramer.

'Is that so?' questioned Tamara coldly. 'I was hoping to hear that he had fallen down on it.'

Carol frowned, then smiled hesitantly. 'You are joking?'

Tamara realised she was giving away something that was very private and very personal between her and Kiel, so she dragged up another smile. 'Of course I am. I'll go and sit in my father's office.' She still couldn't think of it as Kiel's. 'Don't tell Kiel I'm here, I'd like to surprise him.'

'Can I bring you a cup of tea?'

Tamara shook her head. 'Nothing, thank you.'

Ben Wilding's office had always been comfortable and familiar, old-fashioned even, filled with the smell of his brier pipe. As a child Tamara had loved to swivel on his chair, swinging white-socked legs that had not quite reached the floor, dreaming of the day when she would head the company. It had been a lifelong dream.

Until now! Her head jerked sharply, her eyes disbelieving as they skimmed the room. She could have been on a different planet. Gone was her father's antique oak desk, gone was the leather armchair with the brass studs, gone was the worn and faded Axminster carpet. In their place was total anonymity.

Cool greys and chromium-plated steel. A glass-topped desk, no less, with an uncomfortable-looking grey tweed chair. Pen and ink drawings in chromium frames against plain grey walls. Square grey filing cabinets, a square grey computer on the desk. It was an angular room, a workmanlike room. It did not encourage friendly conversation. Say what you've got to say and then get out, was the message that came across. Tamara wondered if all the other employees felt the same?

Her father had always prided himself on his excellent relationship with his work people. If they had any complaints or worries or suggestions they were free to come and see him at any time. He would sit them down and listen and talk to them as though they were his closest friends. She was horrified by this grotesque transformation.

'Well, what do you think?'

The hairs on the back of Tamara's neck rose at the sound of the well-remembered voice and it took her a few seconds to compose herself and turn around. Her cool, beautiful brown eyes met equally cool, clear grey ones. There was an instant of thinly veiled hostility before she said, 'Actually I think it's appalling. It offends my senses. You've left none of my father's identity.'

'What is done is done,' Kiel Kramer said coldly, moving across to the impersonal desk, tossing his jacket on to the back of a tubular chrome chair as he did so. He had not changed. He was still as self-assured and insufferably arrogant as he had ever been.

She had seen him briefly at her father's funeral and before that when his sister had died over a year earlier, but not at all in between. His face had surprisingly matured in that short space of time; she could see lines where none had been before, but it simply added to rather than detracted from his undeniable sexuality. A part of him that she chose to ignore.

His dark brown hair was cropped short and was as strictly controlled as his life. His jutting brows angled over grey eyes that seemed to be perpetually narrowed. His strong, straight nose flared at the nostrils and his mouth was compressed, hiding the sensual fullness that she knew was there. His jawline was square and aggressively male, and as he stood facing her, long brown fingers resting lightly on the desk in front of him, his whole stance spelt danger.

'I've been expecting you,' he said, his eyes insolently and slowly and thoroughly roving the full length of her body in its short, black, ultra-feminine designer dress. He missed not one inch of her anatomy, lingering on the swell of her breasts, the suggestive V of her neckline, her long, shapely legs.

Tamara suffered his appraisal with coolly arched brows and a disdainful expression. 'In that case,' she replied, 'I'll come straight to the point. I want you out of here. I don't care that my father left you this business, I'll buy it off you. It was always understood that one day it would be mine. I can't think why he changed his mind—unless someone did it for him?' She looked pointedly into the slate-hard greyness of his eyes and the room filled with tension and hatred so tangible that she felt it choking her, entering her lungs, forcing her to gasp for air.

'And you think you could run things single-handed and still do the designing?'

'I'd have a jolly good try,' she told him firmly.

'From my point of view we are both needed here.'

'This is a family company, Kiel.' Or it had been until her father had made this crazy decision. She felt sure Kiel had had something to do with it.

'Aren't I almost one of the family?'

His mocking smile set her teeth on edge, but unfortunately, where her father was concerned, this had been true. She had never shared his feelings, though. Kiel had been a part of her life for as long as she could remember and she had always resented him. Sometimes she had even felt that her father had thought more of Kiel than he did her.

'Rest assured, Kiel Kramer,' she said tightly, 'that I have no intention of taking orders from you.'

'Really?' He moved round to the front of the desk, leaning back against it, his eyes resting unnervingly on her face. When he spoke his voice was icy cold. 'As far as I'm concerned it will give me the opportunity to get a little of my own back.' A moment's threatening silence, and then, 'Have you any idea how I've suffered because of you?'

'You're still holding me responsible for Anna's death?' Tamara asked in faint disbelief.

'To my own death,' he announced dramatically.

She swung away, faintly apprehensive, though she was damned if she would let him see it. She had never told him the true facts of the situation. Much as she hated the man, she did not want to ruin the perfect image he had of his delicate sister. The bond between them had been truly remarkable.

At the age of ten, Anna had clung to him when their parents had died. Kiel, ten years older, had assumed the role not many young men of his age would care to consider, putting his sister's happiness before his own, teaching her, guiding her, protecting her— protecting her too much in fact, though he had never known that. And were she to tell him now he would not believe it.

'I've shocked you, eh?'

The deep, resonant tones of Kiel's voice made Tamara turn quickly, and as she did so her long black hair swung forward over her shoulder. She brushed it back impatiently.

'Allow me.' With incredibly gentle fingers he lifted the few strands of hair that still clung to the soft wool of her dress and stroked them back into place. For a couple of seconds his hand rested on her nape and Tamara felt a tingle run right through the heart of her, and images of another time, another world, flashed into her mind, but she ignored them and stepped back. 'It's an empty threat. I don't believe a word of it.'

His brows rose and there was a warning light in his eyes. 'That would be a mistake.'

Tamara's mouth firmed. 'You don't intimidate me, Kiel Kramer. There isn't room for both of us here, especially if you're adopting that sort of attitude. I shall find some way to get rid of you.'

He smiled thinly. 'Then it looks as though we shall have an unholy battle on our hands. Now, if you've said all you came to say I'd be obliged if you'd leave.' He moved round to the other side of the desk and sat down, straightening a photograph of Anna and his parents, making a pretence of sorting some papers. 'I'm very busy.'

Doing what had once been her father's work! Which should now be hers! Tamara walked swiftly across to the door, holding down her boiling anger with difficulty. 'I shall be here at nine prompt in the morning, Kiel, and there's only one of us can be in charge.'

Kiel's threat brought back unhappy memories for Tamara. His sister's death just over a year ago had been an unfortunate accident and it had taken every ounce of Tamara's courage to get back behind the wheel of a car again.

It should never have happened. If she hadn't gone to that party with Anna. If Anna had not resisted her when she'd tried to drag her away. If Anna hadn't continued to fight her when they'd been in the car. *If, if, if.* The tiny word had a lot to answer for.

As Tamara waited at a set of traffic-lights she saw in her mind's eye the whirling greenery as the car swerved off the road. The tree rushing towards them. The moment of impact. The crunching of metal. Anna's screams as she sailed through the windscreen. The silence. The last shuddering sighs of the mutilated car.

Tamara had worn her seatbelt, Anna had refused. Tamara had had to be cut out of the car, but she had been alive. Anna had died.

The sound of car horns mingled with the pictures in her mind and Tamara realised with a start that the traffic-lights had changed to green. Her hands were trembling as she put the car into gear, her palms moist as she gripped the wheel. And when she arrived home and dragged herself out of the car her legs threatened to buckle beneath her.

She stood a moment before entering the house, regulating her breathing, telling herself that it was insanity letting Kiel Kramer affect her like this. But it wasn't just him. It was the memories he had resurrected. He did not know the nightmares she had suffered for weeks after the accident.

And that night they came back. She woke bathed in sweat and sat bolt upright. They had hit the tree again and again, each time an action replay, each time Anna dying. It was hideous; it was gruesome; she couldn't stand it.

She would not let herself fall asleep again in case the nightmare returned, and she rose early, determined to be in the office before Kiel. The Jewellery Quarter itself was a maze of streets, rows and rows of Victorian terraced houses converted into workshops, many manufacturers selling directly to the public. Some of the buildings were new, purpose-built for the trade. There was a jewellery school where all the skills were taught, the Assay Office where the hallmarking took place, pubs, banks, the *British Jeweller* magazine had its publishing house there—it was a completely self-contained community.

In a prominent position stood the green and gold Chamberlain clock, erected in 1903 in honour of the

Right Hon Joseph Chamberlain MP, known as the Guardian Angel of the Jewellery Quarter for the work he had done in abolishing plate duty. It said a quarter to nine exactly when Tamara arrived, but even so Kiel was there before her. His red Mercedes occupied the position where her father used to park his Ford Granada, and Tamara learned from Brenda, their receptionist, that he was in at eight every morning.

Wilding Jewellery occupied a corner position. Three steps led to wide double glass doors and the semi-hexagon-shaped reception area was carpeted in a soft dove-grey. Showcases displayed selected pieces of jewellery. Their main market was independent, high-class jewellers in London and other major cities throughout the world. Most of their work was made to order.

A door in the corner of the reception area led through to the workshops and upstairs were the offices. There was also a back door to the premises from the car park but Tamara rarely used it, preferring to go in the main entrance. It always gave her a thrill to see on display the jewellery she had lovingly and carefully designed.

The mounters, polishers and setters were already at work; they started at eight. Perhaps this was why Kiel had decided to go in at eight as well?

The offices, set along one side of the premises, looked down over the workshop. Kiel's room was at the very end of the corridor, and could also be reached by a second staircase. Next was Carol's, then Tamara's own, and lastly the small general office where a girl looked after the accounts and did anything else that was asked of her.

As Tamara walked along the corridor Kiel appeared in his open doorway, almost as though he had been listening for her arrival. 'When you've taken off your coat I'd like a word,' he said peremptorily, and disappeared inside.

Tamara felt swift anger surge. Already he was throwing around his orders. She flung down her coat and marched straight in. The grey, geometrical furniture was as much a shock this time as it had been before and she gave a shudder of distaste as she entered.

Kiel was standing looking down at the men working below and she wondered how much of his time he spent there, and what effect it was having on them. They were a good team who worked well together, but she knew they would resent being watched over like this.

Several seconds went by before he turned, yet Tamara knew he must have heard her enter. When he did his cool grey eyes were expressionless, his mouth firm. 'Let's get one thing clear straight away—I'm in charge here.'

Tamara opened her mouth, knowing he was referring to her parting shot yesterday, but before she could speak he went on, 'It may interest you to know that I have several new shops interested in one-off pieces of jewellery. Apparently you've made quite a name for yourself as a designer. You're going to be so busy you won't have time for anything else.'

Tamara eyed him mutinously. 'You've done this deliberately, haven't you?'

'Tried to get business, yes,' he answered smoothly. 'I have several contacts; it seems a pity not to use them. Already the orders are pouring in.'

'That's not what I mean and you know it,' she snapped.

'You should be pleased that trade is improving. I know Ben had quite a lucrative business here, but it's nowhere near reached its full potential. Some of his business methods were pretty old-fashioned.'

'You don't have to tell me that, Kiel Kramer, I already know. I had some pretty good ideas myself, but for some reason my father wouldn't listen.' She waited for the derogatory comment, but instead he nodded as though he understood, and that was worse. 'If you have any more ideas,' she snapped. 'I'd like you to talk them over with me first. Maybe my father did hand the company over to you, but I'm still his daughter and I think that gives me as much of a say as you.'

'You want the pleasure of vetoing every suggestion I make?'

'Only if I don't agree.'

'Which I imagine,' he said drily, 'will be ninety-nine times out of a hundred. I have no illusions, Tamara, about the way your mind works.'

Her chin lifted haughtily. 'How can I help it when you've been a thorn in my side for the whole of my life?'

'Things did not have to be like that between us.'

'No?' Her wide brown eyes fixed on him coldly. 'Was I supposed to welcome you as a surrogate brother? Wasn't I supposed to mind that my father lavished as much, if not more, love and attention on you than he did on me?'

'I think you're exaggerating, Tamara.'

'You don't know how deeply it hurt me,' she defended. Maybe, as a child, she had read more into it than there had been, but it was too late for her to alter her opinion of Kiel. Her resentment was buried deep inside her and there it would remain for the rest of her life.

'It's not up to me to apologise for your father's behaviour,' he said. 'I'm deeply appreciative of all he's done for me over the years. I didn't ask for any of it.'

But he had got it all the same, and bitterness washed over her as she made for the door. It grieved her to concede that he was the boss, but there was nothing she could do about it. Between them, Kiel and her father had run her into a corner. She wondered how long they had been hatching this little plot up between them. Before her father's illness? Before she went to Japan? Had it been on the cards for years?

In her own office she reached out the bulging file of notes and sketches she had made in Japan, and glanced through the various enquiries that had landed on her desk while she had been away. Business had been fairly quiet after the pre-Christmas rush, and she had not felt guilty about taking so much time off, but now it looked as though she was going to be working flat out for the next few months, and it galled her to think that Kiel was the one who had drummed up the new business.

A tap on her door heralded Carol. 'I've just made Kiel a cup of coffee; would you like one?'

Tamara nodded. 'Please.'

In less than a minute Carol was back with two cups and she sat herself down, looking as though she was prepared for a cosy tête-à-tête, which in itself was unusual. Carol was an attractive girl with short, copper-tinted hair cut in a geometrical bob. She was slim and tall but tended to be too serious.

At this moment, however, there was a becoming glow to her cheeks and a brilliance to her eyes that had never been there before. She had the look of a woman in love. Tamara wondered whether Kiel was aware of Carol's feelings.

'What can you tell me about Kiel?' Carol asked, leaning forward eagerly, getting straight on with the subject dearest to her heart. 'You know him well, don't you? Isn't he a friend of your family?'

Tamara shrugged. 'I've known him all my life, yes, but he was more a friend of my father's than mine. What do you want to know about him?'

'For starters, is he married?' asked Carol quickly.

'No.'

Relief flooded the girl's face. 'Has he a steady girlfriend?'

'Not that I'm aware of.'

'I can't believe it,' said Carol. 'He's so marvellously good-looking. Why hasn't some girl snapped him up?'

'He looked after his sister until fairly recently. I suppose he never had time.'

Carol took a sip of her coffee. 'How do you think I could make him notice me? He seems not to even realise I'm human. I'm like another one of his blessed pieces of office equipment.'

'You hate it too?' asked Tamara with a smile.

Carol nodded.

'It's awful, isn't it? I wonder who advised him.'

'It was his own choice,' confessed Carol. 'He ticked the items in a catalogue and told me to order them.'

'I wish you'd told him what a ghastly mistake he was making. It's so—impersonal.'

'Like Kiel,' said Carol.

Not always, thought Tamara, but she had no intention of telling Carol that Kiel had once held her in his arms and kissed her. It had been quite a moment and, even though at the time she had not welcomed his embrace, it had left its impression on her, and she had thought about that kiss often over the last ten years.

The phone rang in Carol's office and the girl reluctantly left, and Tamara's mind went winging back to the episode when she had been just eighteen.

Kiel had been working abroad and she had not seen him for over three years. She had been dressed ready to go to a party when he'd knocked on the door, and before she could stop him he had walked into the house. She'd deeply resented his familiarity, but her father had always made him welcome so there was nothing she could do about it.

'My parents are out,' she said haughtily, following him into their lounge. As a child she had always thought him a giant of a man because he was taller than either of her parents, but now she was grown up herself she did not find him so intimidating, and felt that at last she could hold her own with him.

'That's a pity; this is only a flying visit.'

'You should have phoned. I'm sure my father would have stayed in if he'd known you were coming.' Tamara was unable to hide her sarcasm.

'I'm sure he would,' said Kiel, raising a brow at her tone.

'And I hope you're not going to stay long because I'm going out too.'

'So I gathered.' His eyes flickered briefly over the pert thrust of her breasts which announced her womanhood. Her dress had a black, strapless bodice and a short, purple, tiered skirt. 'You've certainly grown up, Tamara. You were a child three years ago, now you're a young lady. But I don't like your hair like that—it doesn't suit you.'

Tamara had spent hours pinning it up on top of her head in elaborate curls. She thought it made her look sophisticated and was really pleased with the result. 'I didn't ask for your opinion,' she said shortly, a little nervous about the way he was looking at her.

He moved closer, and before Tamara could stop him he had pulled out a couple of the pins. Her hair came tumbling down in deep waves over her shoulders. 'That's better,' he said softly. 'Are you going to do the rest, or shall I?' His hand was resting against her nape and she could smell his aftershave, and breathing became suddenly difficult.

For a few seconds she eyed him in confusion. This was a Kiel she did not know and something was happening to her own body that she had not expected either. His hand behind her neck pulled her slowly towards him. 'You're a very attractive girl, Tamara.' His voice was low and mesmeric and his hand slid over her bare shoulders, feeling the innocent softness of her skin.

Tamara knew she ought to move but she felt somehow hypnotised, until suddenly he lowered his head and his mouth came down on hers. She was galvanised into action, her hands pushing hard against his chest, her eyes flashing. 'Get away from me, you brute. What are you doing? Daddy will kill you if he finds out.'

'I won't tell him if you don't,' he mocked. 'What's wrong? Have you never been kissed before?'

'Not by an old man!' she yelled.

'I'm only twenty-six, Tamara.' He smiled.

'That *is* old,' she snapped. 'Just get away from me, keep away, I hate you!'

Throughout her whole life he had mercilessly teased her, which she had hated, and now this. Her whole being was filled with an emotion she could not understand. She liked the feelings he had awoken in her, yet at the same time she was embarrassed by them and loathed him for creating them.

He chuckled. 'One day you'll change your mind.'

But she had kept her feelings tightly locked away, affecting disinterest whenever they had met, and after the accident, when he'd blamed her for his sister's death, she had been glad she had never let him see that she found him attractive.

Tamara immersed herself in her work and forgot the time, totally surprised when Kiel strode into her office and announced it was lunchtime. 'There are things we should discuss,' he said peremptorily. 'We'll do it while we eat.'

Tamara frowned. 'I don't want to go anywhere with you.'

'I'm talking about having it here,' he corrected her tersely. 'I've already ordered sandwiches. Come through to my office in a few minutes.'

She felt like ignoring his request—she did not want to lunch with him, and could not imagine what it was he wanted to discuss. But curiosity finally got the better of her.

'Sit down,' he said, placing a plate of prawn and mayonnaise sandwiches in front of her. He had shed the jacket to his grey suit and his sleeves were rolled up to the elbows. The hairs on his arms glinted gold in the stripes of sunlight that came through his half-closed vertical blinds.

For a few seconds he did not speak. He took a bite out of his wholemeal bread sandwich and surveyed her lazily, and to her dismay Tamara felt the full impact of his sexuality. His grey eyes were compelling and she was unable to look away. 'What am I doing here?' she demanded, annoyed by her response, annoyed that feelings she had so carefully locked away had suddenly surfaced. She made no attempt to touch her sandwiches. How could she eat in the enemy camp? And he was still her enemy, no matter that her body was proving to be a traitor.

'I have a very exciting enquiry and I want to discuss it with you before I make any sort of commitment.'

Her finely arched brows rose. 'You're deferring to me?' This was unbelievable.

He smiled slowly and contemptuously. 'Not exactly. You didn't really think I'd do that, did you? But I need to know whether it's beyond your capabilities.'

Tamara gasped her indignation. 'Nothing is beyond me.'

'Good, then read this.' He pushed a piece of paper over his desk towards her.

Tamara's eyes widened as she skimmed the typewritten lines. They were being commissioned to design and make a necklace and earrings for Princess Margherita Maria of Italy!

CHAPTER TWO

'THIS is incredible,' said Tamara breathlessly. 'How did Princess Margherita hear about us?' Nothing like this had ever happened in her father's day.

'I happen to know certain people in the right quarters,' Kiel admitted. 'I mentioned I had now taken over your father's company, and the fact that his daughter was a brilliant designer, and it seems to have worked. What do you think?'

'It's wonderful, it's the most marvellous opportunity,' she gasped, resenting only the fact that Kiel had obtained such an important commission and not her father. 'But I don't know the sort of things the Princess likes, or doesn't like, or what she normally wears, or anything at all about her. I might design something that's totally unsuitable.'

'You're saying you don't want to do it? That you're not capable?' Hard grey eyes bored into hers.

Tamara frowned quickly. 'No, I'm not. This is the best thing that's ever happened. Of course I'll have a go.'

Kiel nodded. 'I thought you might.'

It would involve a great deal of research to find out exactly what Princess Margherita liked, thought Tamara, her adrenalin high, but the prestige afterwards would more than outweigh all the time and effort spent.

'I can't eat,' she said, pushing her plate away. 'I must get on.' Her workload was already high, and now this. She wouldn't have a minute to breathe.

24

Already her mind was running on. Perhaps some of the ideas she'd had while in Japan?

'Nonsense,' said Kiel. 'You need to eat to keep up your energy. Don't you like prawns? Shall I send for something else?'

'Yes, I like them,' replied Tamara, 'but——'

'Then eat,' he insisted sternly.

And Tamara was forced to swallow them down while he watched, which made her feel very uncomfortable. He had no idea that, sitting close to him like this, she found it totally impossible to ignore his sexuality. Even though there was an air of tension between them and he was making it very clear that he despised her, it made no difference.

Afterwards she made coffee, glad to escape for a few minutes, and when she brought it into his office Kiel was once again standing watching the men.

'I don't think they'll like you doing that,' she said before she could stop herself.

He swung around, frowning. 'Doing what?'

'Watching them work.'

'I've ordered some new machinery.'

'You've what?' gasped Tamara, putting down the two cups and staring at him incredulously. 'My father prided himself that every single piece of jewellery leaving this workshop was handmade. It was his reputation. What are you planning—mass production for the cheaper end of the market?'

He looked at her scathingly. 'Of course not. With modern machinery techniques it's possible to manufacture more accurately and perhaps even more quickly.'

Tamara knew he was right; she had tried often enough in the past to persuade her father to make changes. But it still annoyed her to think that Kiel

was so much more go-ahead and was wasting no time
in changing over to high technology. 'What do Bill
and the rest of them think?' Bill Pearce had been with
her father ever since he'd set up. He was a master
craftsman.

Kiel shrugged. 'I met with some opposition.'

'But I've no doubt you managed to persuade them
that it will be for the best?' she countered drily.

'Naturally. And when I offered them a rise to go
with it I had no more complaints.'

'You do realise you'll lose valuable time while
they're learning how to use the various machines
you're installing?'

'I have a training course organised.'

Tamara eyed him coldly. 'You've thought of everything, haven't you?'

'I hope so.'

It was said with such smugness that she could have
thrown her coffee at him. 'You seem to have ac-
complished an awful lot in the short time you've been
here,' she crisped.

'And I intend instigating many more changes,' he
told her bluntly.

Tamara picked up her coffee and drank it quickly.
'Thank you for the lunch. I'll get back to work.'

Her anger was only sour grapes, she realised that.
He was doing things she would have done herself, had
she been left in control. That was why it hurt so much.
And because he hated her, he was taking great delight
in flaunting his immediate success.

Kiel did not detain her as she walked from the room,
merely watching her through narrowed eyes. Tamara
felt every nerve in her body prickle. It was going to
be hell working for this man.

For the next two hours Tamara tossed ideas backwards and forwards in her mind, finally going down to the workshop to have a word with Bill. She knew what could or could not be done, as she had trained as a jeweller herself and was experienced in working with different precious metals, but she always consulted Bill before committing ideas to paper.

She was not concerned with the commissioned jewellery yet, there were too many other urgent orders that needed attention, but she had to get through as many as she could to give herself time to concentrate solely on this very special order.

She stood a moment and watched Bill as he domed a small sheet of gold that he had already cut to the size he wanted. It was placed over the correct-sized hollow in his doming block, a punch held in position over it, and then repeatedly tapped with a hammer until it followed the shape of the depression.

He looked up when he had finished, a thin, energetic man with balding grey hair and a kindly face. 'It's good to see you back, Tammy. Your father's sorely missed. He was the best there is.'

'I miss him too, Bill. I loved him so very, very much. What do you think of Mr Kramer?'

'He's all right,' he admitted quietly, 'though some of the men don't like him. He's a typical new brush with the changes he's making. I always thought you'd take over if anything happened to Ben.'

'So did I.' Her mouth twisted angrily as she spoke. 'But apparently I'm of more use in other ways.'

'And so you are,' said Bill, smiling. 'I hear we've got more orders than ever, so it looks as if your father's choice might be a good one after all.'

'Time will tell,' she said sharply.

Bill's faded blue eyes widened at her crisp tone. 'You don't approve of——?' He nodded his head towards Kiel's office.

Tamara wondered whether he was standing there watching them, but she resisted the urge to look up. 'Not really. But as you say, it looks as though he's going to be good for the company. What do you think of his ideas for new machinery?'

Bill shrugged. 'We'll get used to it, I reckon. Your father was a bit slow to move with the times.'

Tamara silently applauded his attitude.

'Exactly who is this Kiel Kramer?' asked Bill. 'Rumour has it he was a personal friend of Ben's. Is that so? He's a bit young, I thought.'

'He's my father's godson, actually,' replied Tamara. 'The son he never had.' She did not realise how bitterly she had added those words until Bill looked at her curiously. 'It's true,' she defended. 'Kiel's parents died and my father adopted him in all but name. Will you take a look at these sketches?' And the subject of Kiel Kramer was closed.

But as she lay in bed that night Tamara recalled a conversation she'd had with her father a few weeks before she'd gone to Japan. He had said he wanted her to know exactly why he thought so much of Kiel. Perhaps he had been trying to hint at what he was going to do? If only she had known.

'When I was a young man,' her father had said, 'long before I met your mother, I fell in love with the most beautiful girl in the world.' He smiled softly at the memory. 'But before I plucked up the courage to propose she ran off and married my best friend.'

'Oh, no, how awful.' Tamara recalled her response as vividly as on the day he had told her.

'Her name was Kathy,' her father went on slowly. 'My friend's name was Alan Kramer.'

'Kiel's parents?' she gasped.

'That's right. I was devastated. But gradually, over the weeks and the months, I came to my senses. If that was what Kathy wanted, if she loved Alan more than she loved me, then the least I could do was be happy for her. My love for her was selfless, I wanted her happiness before my own.'

'Oh, Daddy.' Tamara remembered going down on her knees in front of him, taking his hands, her eyes wide and sad. 'How you must have suffered.'

He nodded and swallowed a lump in his throat. 'Eventually I was able to go and see them and hold out the hand of friendship, and when Kiel was born twelve months later and they asked me to be his godfather, I was flattered and pleased. I suppose I took more than a normal interest in the boy—all I could think of was that if I'd married Kathy he could have been mine.'

Tamara nodded. 'I wish you'd told me this before, Daddy.'

'I didn't think you were old enough to understand.'

'I would have been,' she protested, but maybe he was right. 'How about Mummy?' she asked then. 'Does she know about Kathy?'

'Oh, yes,' he said. 'I've kept nothing from her. In fact after Kathy left me I didn't think I'd ever fall in love again. Kiel was almost three when I met your mother, and I'd watched him grow with almost parental pride. Hilary was nothing like Kathy, of course, but I realised I was in love again after all that time. We got married and four years later you came along. Kiel was eight then.'

'And you'd have preferred me to be a boy?' asked Tamara softly.

He closed his eyes and his head fell forward to hide his guilt. 'I can't deny it, Tamara. I was terribly disappointed, but I consoled myself with the fact that the next one might be a boy. But, as you know, there were no more. Never think for one minute, though, that I don't love you, Tamara. I always have, very much. You've been a constant source of pleasure and pride to me.'

His hands gripped hers so tightly that they hurt and it was a few minutes before he spoke again. 'When you were two years old Anna was born. I don't think they'd planned to have any more. Kathy had a difficult pregnancy and, as you know, Anna was never a well child.'

Tamara nodded.

'And Kiel wanted nothing to do with her. You can imagine how a ten-year-old boy felt about a baby sister. The rest you know. Anna was only ten when Kathy and Alan were killed in a plane crash. I wanted Kiel and Anna to come and live with us but Kiel refused. At twenty he thought he was man enough to run the house and look after his sister. His feelings for her changed overnight.'

'He protected her too much,' said Tamara.

Ben nodded. 'It was understandable.'

But his protection had been the indirect cause of Anna's death! And because of this Kiel now hated Tamara!

'I'm glad you've told me, Daddy,' she said, but, although she had then understood why her father had loved Kiel so, it did not lessen her resentment now over the business. If he had loved them both as much as he had said he had, why hadn't he left it to them jointly? Even that would have been better than her feeling left out altogether. Admittedly, he had left her some money—a quite considerable amount—but what was that compared with owning and running the firm she had grown up with?

During the next few days Kiel left Tamara severely alone. Whether it was deliberate or coincidental she did not know, but in any event it was a blessing in disguise.

Frequently she saw him down in the workshop talking to the men, and once he looked up and saw her watching him from her window. His mock salute irritated her and she made sure that he never caught her looking at him again.

Tamara was looking forward to the weekend. She hadn't seen her friend, Patti, in ages, and had arranged to go over to her house so that she could catch up on what had been happening while she had been away. Then on Saturday morning her mother told her that she was giving a dinner party that evening and wanted her to help get it ready.

'A dinner party?' Tamara queried with a frown. It seemed strange when her mother was still in mourning.

'That's right,' said Hilary Wilding firmly. 'I'm going away for a few weeks, and I've invited Bill because of his loyalty to your father all these years, and Kiel because I think the two men ought to get to know one another on a personal level. Your father would have wanted me to do it.'

'And I suppose you want me to make up the numbers?' asked Tamara with a sinking heart. 'It doesn't matter that I've arranged to go out?'

'Only to Patti's,' said her mother quietly. 'You can easily put her off. I'd like you to do this, Tamara, for me.'

'Of course, Mummy; and you said something about going away.' Her frown returned. 'Where? Isn't it rather sudden?'

Hilary shook her head. 'Not really, I've been thinking about it ever since...' She tailed off and wiped a tear from her eye. 'I'm going to Ida's. I need a complete change of scenery.'

'I understand,' said Tamara softly. Ida Bronsey was her mother's sister, widowed a few years earlier. They would be good company for one another. 'But I'm going to miss you.'

While in Japan Tamara had bought a black silk kimono-style dress, delicately embroidered with silver thread, and she wore it that evening with black silk stockings and high-heeled patent leather mules. In her ears she hung a pair of long, silver filigree earrings studded with tiny pieces of black onyx, and in defiance of teenage memories she piled her hair high on top of her head.

Kiel arrived first, a few minutes before eight. He smiled coolly into her eyes and Tamara took him straight through into the dining-room, doing her best to hide the flutter of awareness he provoked in his immaculate off-white suit. On some men it would have looked all wrong, but on Kiel it was devastatingly perfect, and, heavens, she must be foolish to feel anything at all for this man.

The table was laid with her mother's best Wedgwood china and Waterford crystal. In the centre, arranged in a champagne glass, were deep blue grape hyacinths and palest lemon primroses, still damp from the garden.

'Aren't they beautiful?' she asked, feeling the need to break the silence that was settling uncomfortably around them.

He gave them no more than a cursory glance. 'Very nice, but no more stunning than you look yourself. Am I to assume you've dressed up for me?'

Tamara gave him a sweetly innocent smile which did not deceive Kiel for one moment. 'But of course. And for Bill. Where is he? He should be here now.'

As if on cue the doorbell rang again and, excusing herself, she hurried to open it. Bill looked smarter than she had ever seen him, in a navy suit and white shirt. 'This is a rare honour,' he said, looking slightly embarrassed.

'My mother felt you deserved it.'

'She didn't have to,' he said.

'Kiel's here too.'

His brows rose quickly and she knew he was re-calling their conversation a few days ago.

'My mother thought it would be nice for you to meet your new boss socially. Come on through, I'll get you a drink.' How much easier she found it to talk to Bill.

Hilary had joined Kiel and the four of them stood talking and sipping sherry, and Tamara was able to look at Kiel unobserved while he spoke to her mother. His raw sexuality was something she had only just discovered and it disturbed her more than she cared to admit. Although she had felt the power of him all those years ago, it had certainly never been anything like as strong as this, unless she had been too naïve to understand her feelings. Or was it that memory had faded over the years? He had moved out of their lives for quite a while and she hadn't seen very much of him.

'Is something wrong?' he asked suddenly and quietly.

Tamara's cheeks coloured—an event unusual in itself. 'Should there be?'

'You're looking at me as though you've never seen me before.'

She was tempted to say that she wished she never had seen him, ever, but out of respect for her mother and Bill she smiled quietly. 'I'm sorry, I didn't realise I was staring.'

Although it was supposed to be a social evening, the conversation over dinner inevitably turned to what was dearest to all their hearts—the jewellery trade— and the new machinery Kiel was installing. Tamara grew silent, listening to the men's animated discussion. This was the business side of Kiel which she was growing to resent more and more. He had taken her place in the company and there was no way she was ever going to accept that.

She deliberately ignored the traitorous way her body was behaving, the heat that pervaded her skin whenever she met the deliberately sensual message in his eyes. She knew it was all an act put on for her mother's benefit. Kiel wasn't interested in her, and he'd have the biggest shock of his life if he knew the sort of response he was evoking.

He sat opposite her at the table and she watched as he forked food into his mouth. His hands were long-fingered and neatly manicured, his square jaw clean-shaven, his hair freshly trimmed. He was courteous, polite and friendly towards her, more so than he had ever been before. But on Monday they would be enemies again; she knew that as surely as if he had told her.

'What do you think, Tamara?'

She suddenly realised that she was being spoken to and had not heard one word of their conversation.

'I'm sorry,' she said. 'I was miles away. What were you saying?'

'Kiel suggested that we hire another setter,' said Bill.

Suddenly she was alert, very much so, and a swift frown creased her brow. 'Why?'

'With the new machinery the mounts will be made so much quicker,' pointed out Kiel tersely, catching the doubt and disbelief in Tamara's tone.

'But don't you think you ought to wait and see whether Paul and the others can cope before you start anyone else?' She was glad Bill had brought her into the conversation. He clearly felt equally as uneasy about it.

'If we wait too long we could lose out,' said Kiel. 'Sam's free to start straight away, having just returned from a job abroad. I don't think we should hang fire. Good setters are becoming increasingly scarce.'

Tamara privately thought he was running ahead of himself, but she knew it would make no difference what she said. She lifted her shoulders in an indifferent shrug. 'It really has nothing to do with me any more.'

'That's right, it hasn't,' said Kiel with a disarming smile which didn't fool her for one second. Nevertheless, his smile softened the harsh lines of his face, revealing very white, slightly uneven teeth, and she suddenly wished that she had met him in different circumstances. There was a whole side to Kiel she had never discovered and she found herself wondering what he would be like as a lover. Her body grew warm at the thought and she was glad he couldn't read her mind. It was foolishness thinking like this when they were never likely to be anything other than enemies.

They finished the superb raspberry mousse and her mother suggested they take their coffee into the drawing-room. 'You two young people go on in. Bill will help me bring in the coffee, won't you, Bill?'

Bill grinned and nodded and got up straight away. Despite Hilary's good intentions, he seemed out of his depth with Kiel. Her father had treated Bill as an equal—in fact they had been equals, being contemporaries—but it was clear that he would never regard Kiel in any other way than as the new boss of the company. He would never develop the same rapport he'd had with her father. He had never been afraid to voice his opinions or make suggestions and Ben had always listened. She couldn't see Kiel doing that. Kiel wanted to run things his way.

When Kiel sat down beside her Tamara abruptly got up. But he caught her wrist and hissed fiercely, 'For your mother's benefit I've done my best to keep things running smoothly this evening. Don't you think you should do the same?'

She eyed him belligerently and then subsided. For her mother's sake.

'I'd like to take you out to lunch tomorrow.'

Her eyes shot wide in surprise and her chin lifted fractionally. 'To please my mother? No, thank you. Spending time with you is hardly my idea of pleasure, no matter what she might think.'

Kiel's eyes hardened for an instant but he kept his smile. 'I'll pick you up at about twelve. We'll go somewhere for lunch and then perhaps——'

'Don't waste your breath,' she cut in savagely. 'I'm seeing a friend tomorrow. I already cancelled my plans for this evening because of you. I don't intend to do it again.'

His brows lifted. 'A boyfriend? I wasn't aware that you had one.'

'I don't see that it's any business of yours,' she said icily, 'but, as a matter of fact, no. It's Patti Woods. You probably know her. We used to go to school together.'

He smiled. 'Yes, I remember—Fatty Patti. Isn't that what they called her?'

Tamara inclined her head. 'But you wouldn't recognise her now. She's as slim as me and very beautiful.'

'Is that so? How remarkable. Perhaps I should meet this changed creature.'

'I doubt she'd want anything to do with you,' replied Tamara crossly, though she knew this was a wildly inaccurate statement. Patti had never actually met Kiel, but she had seen him in passing and heard enough about him to be madly enthusiastic. And when Tamara had phoned and said he was the new owner of her father's company, Patti had gone ecstatic.

Her mother and Bill came in at that moment and Hilary Wilding frowned when she saw the grim look on her daughter's face. 'Is something wrong?'

'A slight difference of opinion,' answered Kiel for her. 'A good healthy argument. It's forgotten now. Isn't that right, Tamara?'

He smiled into her eyes and placed his hand on top of hers, and Tamara could not help feeling a *frisson* of pleasure. He really had beautiful eyes. Maybe she had never noticed them properly before? Or was it that they had always been as cold as ice? Now they were like the soft velvet of a dove's wing, suggesting an intimacy that did not exist.

She swallowed hard and nodded. 'Shall I pour the coffee?' What the hell was happening that he could do this to her? she asked herself angrily. She did not want to be affected by this man. Not now, not ever.

'It's all right, love, I'll do it,' said her mother. 'Pass Kiel the mints.'

Was it an accident that his fingers touched hers again? This really was taking things too far. What was he trying to do? She pulled the dish away quickly and offered it to Bill.

Conversation became general and, far earlier than Tamara expected, Kiel announced that he was going. 'Don't bother to get up, Hilary. Tamara can see me out. How about you, Bill? Can I give you a lift?'

'I'll stay a bit longer, if Hilary doesn't mind?' said Bill.

The older woman nodded. 'Of course I don't mind.'

'I've enjoyed the evening and the food was superb, Hilary,' said Kiel. 'It was good of you to go to so much trouble.'

'It's helped take my mind off things,' she admitted, smiling delightedly when Kiel folded her in his arms and gave her a bear-like hug.

Tamara walked down the long hall to the front door and Kiel followed, but he stopped her from opening it, turning her to face him instead. 'Kiel, what——?'

'Forgive me, Tamara,' he said pleasantly, 'but I want to repeat an experiment I made some ten years ago.' And before she could stop him he had pulled her into his arms and his mouth was on hers in a kiss that was nothing like the one he had tried to give her when she had been just eighteen.

At twenty-six he had not been an inexperienced youth, but even so there was a world of difference between this embrace and that one. Although he held her firmly his lips were gentle, brushing hers softly and expertly, intent on arousing a response that he might not get were he to savage her.

On that occasion she had felt an initial response, had felt the first awakening of her innocent young body, but when she had fought him he had let her go. This time her struggles were ineffectual.

One of Kiel's hands was behind her back, the other holding her head. Her hair came tumbling down about her shoulders, and the kiss went on and on, slowly and gradually inducing a reluctant response. There was no denying his expertise. His hand slid from the back of her head, caressing her nape, gentle, feather-light touches, moving to her ears and her jaw-line, until finally his fingertips joined his mouth on her lips.

He pulled down her lower lip and kissed the soft, silken moistness he found inside. Tamara's heart and pulses defied her sanity and ran away with themselves, and as they did so her lips parted and she found herself returning his kiss.

After all the years of remembering one brief kiss, this bore no resemblance to it. She was even able to forget who he was and what he represented and give herself up to the pleasure of the moment. It was insanity, she knew, and probably tomorrow she would regret it, but for the moment...

Then abruptly he lifted his head and looked deep into her eyes. 'Thank you, Tamara.'

'For what?' she snapped, angry with herself already for being so weak and forgetting it was all a game as far as he was concerned.

'Letting me know that you're not as indifferent to me as you make out. Ten years ago I scared you out of your wits, I admit that. I shouldn't have done it. But tonight, Tamara, tonight was totally different. You responded—dare I say it?—instinctively. Almost as though you wanted to be kissed. You've turned into a warmly sensual woman who knows her own body and its power.'

Tamara flashed her eyes haughtily. 'I don't know what you're talking about.'

'I think you do, Tamara. You've a very beautiful body and I cannot deny that you arouse all my basic male instincts.' He threaded his fingers through her hair and pulled her slowly but firmly towards him. 'It's a pity, a very great pity that there is this barrier between us. I think I would enjoy making love to you.'

Tamara could not believe that she was hearing him correctly. This man who professed to hate her was actually saying that he wanted to make love to her! What kind of a monster was he? He had frozen her out of his life when Anna had died. It was only because of her father's will that they were together now.

On the other hand, she had experienced similar feelings herself and she found it difficult to understand why her body should react like this. She did not agree with casual sex, so why this sudden explosion of feeling? Was it that she had never looked at Kiel closely enough to realise what a sensual man he was? But to become lovers simply for sexual gratification was something she would never agree to.

'Let me go, Kiel,' she said bluntly. 'The only way you'll ever make love to me is by force.'

'Which would be no fun at all,' he replied. 'I like my women to be responsive—as you were a moment ago.'

Tamara wished she could deny it. Instead she contented herself with looking coldly into the grey depths of his eyes.

'One day, perhaps,' he mused, and freed his fingers from her hair.

With relief Tamara stepped forward and opened the door. 'Goodnight, Kiel.'

Her obvious eagerness to get rid of him seemed to afford him some amusement. His lips quirked as he said, 'You won't change your mind about tomorrow?'

'Not if you paid me.'

'In that case, I'll see you on Monday morning. Have a good day.'

Tamara was tempted to slam the door, only the fact that her mother would hear and ask questions stopping her. As she made her way back into the drawing-room she tidied her hair, pulling out the rest of the pins, hoping she did not look as dishevelled as she felt. Hilary and Bill were talking about Ben. It was doing her mother good to talk to someone who had known and respected him for as long as she had, and they looked as comfortable as a pair of old slippers. Tamara smiled to herself. 'Would you two mind if I went to bed?'

'No, love, of course not,' said her mother. 'What were you and Kiel arguing about? I had hoped you'd make an effort this evening.'

Had this whole thing been engineered for her benefit? wondered Tamara. Nothing at all to do with Bill's and Kiel's getting to know each other? She hadn't known her mother was so devious. She shrugged dismissively. 'He wanted to take me out tomorrow and I didn't want to go.'

'Oh, Tamara, love,' said Hilary at once, 'you should have gone. Perhaps he's trying to build up a better relationship now you're working together? He certainly seemed to show a lot of interest in you tonight.'

'I've already put Patti off once,' said Tamara firmly. 'I can't do it again. Goodnight, Mummy, goodnight, Bill.'

*   *   *

'I can't believe it,' said Patti as she let her friend into the house. 'You turned down a date with Kiel to come and see me?'

'If you felt about Kiel the way I do then you'd have done the same thing,' Tamara told her firmly. 'How can I be friendly with a man who's snatched my father's business from under my nose?' Even though Patti was her best friend, she had never told her about Kiel's kiss all those years ago, and her fantasies since. 'Besides, the feeling's mutual. He hates my guts.'

'It's such a pity,' said Patti. 'He'd be perfect for you. When you get to our age there aren't many presentable men left.'

'Are you saying that at the grand old age of twenty-eight we're doomed never to get married?' Tamara laughed.

'I sometimes wonder,' said Patti. 'I lost the best years of my life in another body.'

'But look at you now.' A curvy blonde with beautiful green eyes and an outgoing personality!

'Yes, look at me. My own house, a good job, a good figure, but no man. I'm not cut out to be an old maid, Tamara. How about an introduction to Kiel?'

'You must be joking. I wouldn't wish him on my worst enemy.'

'Oh, come on, he can't be all that bad. I think I might come and see you at your office tomorrow and have a look at him for myself. Will he be in during the lunch hour?'

Tamara nodded. 'He's what is known as a work-aholic. He starts an hour before everyone else and stays long after they've gone.'

Patti grimaced, but their conversation turned to other topics and Kiel was forgotten.

* * *

Tamara could not believe her eyes the next morning when she saw that the new setter was female. There were lots of girls coming into the jewellery trade these days, but her father hadn't approved and their own workforce was still all male, and she had naturally assumed that Sam was male, too.

Kiel introduced her as Samantha Sheldon. 'But everyone calls her Sam,' he added with a twinkle in his eyes, and Tamara knew that he had deliberately misled her.

She was a tall, well-proportioned blonde with deep blue eyes and a confident tilt to her head. She was wearing jeans and a T-shirt, but made them look sexy. Shaking Tamara's hand firmly, she said, 'I think I'm going to like working here.'

As she spoke Sam glanced at Kiel, and there was no disguising the love shining out of her eyes. No wonder he had recommended her for the job. Tamara's own eyes grew icy and her mouth firmed. 'If you'll excuse me, I have work to do.'

Kiel followed her up to her office. 'Is there something wrong? Did I detect the green eye of jealousy? Sam's a brilliant setter, quick and accurate; she'll be an asset.'

'For whom?' snapped Tamara, eyeing him coldly. 'As far as I'm concerned only time will tell.'

'As far as you're concerned it doesn't really matter. You have no say around here, Tamara.'

She felt as though he had slapped her in the face and did not know how she managed to hold on to her anger, and as the day progressed it became clear that the rest of the workforce resented Sam too. Kiel hadn't been wrong when he'd sung her praises, but when she tried to tell Paul how to do his job trouble started.

Paul was their chief setter and had been with the company almost as long as Bill, but he lacked Bill's placid temperament. When Tamara went downstairs to consult Bill about a design, Paul came over to her. 'Who the hell does that girl think she is? Is she trying to take over my job?'

'Please, Paul, give her time,' Tamara said with a soothing smile.

'I don't know why she's been set on,' he snarled. 'We don't need her. There isn't enough work.'

'But there soon will be,' she told him. 'And Mr Kramer thought it would be a good idea to start someone now.'

'A personal friend of his, is she?' sneered Paul. 'I've seen the two of them together. What's going on? Why has that Kramer man taken over? We all thought you'd run the company one day.'

'I have enough to do with the designing,' said Tamara firmly. Although she had confided in Bill Pearce, this man was different. Bill could be trusted to hold his tongue; Paul would tell everyone what she said. 'Mr Kramer is doing a very good job. We've never had so many orders.'

Paul reluctantly agreed. 'But we can still cope. We don't need anyone else.'

'Not at the moment,' she agreed, 'but enquiries are flooding in. Mr Kramer thought we should be one jump ahead of ourselves. I'm sure Sam Sheldon will soon fit in. She's probably feeling unsure of herself. Give her time to settle down.'

He muttered something, but it was obvious he did not agree, and when Tamara went back to her office Kiel was waiting for her. 'What were you and Paul talking about?'

She might have known he'd been watching them. She lifted her chin and eyed him boldly. 'Samantha Sheldon.'

He frowned. 'What's wrong?'

'She's not making herself very well liked.'

'And they're bringing their complaints to you?'

'Not really, I just happened to be down there and——'

'And I trust you told Paul to come and see me if he has any problems?'

'No, I didn't.' Their eyes met and locked in silent battle, and Tamara felt the power of him as she never had before. The relationship between them had never been easy, but now he was trying to assume control over her.

His nostrils flared as his eyes blazed into hers. 'In future please refer any complaints to me. And you'd be as well to remember, Tamara, that this is my company now. You have no say at all in the running of it.'

CHAPTER THREE

TAMARA was still fuming at lunchtime when Patti came into her office. She slapped a hand to her brow. 'Oh, lord, I'd forgotten all about you.'

'Does that mean I'm not going to get an introduction to your handsome boss?' said Patti with a grimace.

'It most certainly does. It wouldn't worry me if I didn't speak to him again for the rest of my life.'

'It's that bad?' Patti's green eyes widened. 'Which is his office? I think I might accidentally wander in and——'

'Have your head bitten off,' cut in Tamara acidly. 'If I were you I'd steer clear. He's not worth getting worked up about. My father must have had a brainstorm when he made out his will. Letting Kiel take over was the worst decision he ever made.'

She walked across to her window and stood looking down. Samantha Sheldon was alone, munching sandwiches. The rest of the men had disappeared, which was unusual in itself. They normally all sat together. It didn't take much working out that the new female setter was to blame. Tamara wondered how long it would be before Kiel took pity on her and asked her to join him.

'Things can't be that bad, surely,' said Patti, looking down also. 'Your father must have felt confident the two of you would get on well together.'

46

Tamara sniffed indelicately. 'My father thought the sun shone out of Kiel's eyes. I don't think he noticed that we never hit it off.'

'More likely he chose to ignore it.'

The male voice made them both spin round. Tamara met the icy coldness of Kiel's eyes and heard Patti gasp at her side.

'Do you discuss me with all your friends?' He stood tall and arrogant, his strong, straight nose flared at the nostrils, brows jutting over narrowed eyes.

'Patti was misguided enough to show an interest in you,' she retorted sharply. 'Kiel, meet Patti Woods. Patti, Kiel Kramer.'

His brows lifted and Tamara knew he was mentally recalling the other, plump Patti whom everyone had made fun of. 'I believe I owe you an apology,' he said, taking Patti's hand and holding it firmly, his face suddenly breaking into a smile, revealing his slightly uneven white teeth, turning him into a dangerously attractive man.

Patti frowned, but seemed dumbstruck, unable to take her eyes off his face, and there was no doubt, thought Tamara, that when he chose to be charming he could win over any girl he liked. Including herself! Except that he never, or rarely, turned on the charm for her.

'I spoilt your arrangements on Saturday night,' he reminded the blonde girl.

'Oh, that,' said Patti with an embarrassed laugh. 'Think nothing of it.'

'Perhaps you'd both like to join me for lunch by way of recompense?'

Tamara looked at him sharply, knowing he had only included her out of politeness. 'No, thanks. I'm too busy.'

'I'd love to,' answered Patti at the same time, then laughed awkwardly. 'I'm sorry, I——'

'It looks as though it's just you and me.' Kiel dazzled her with his smile and Patti looked hesitantly at Tamara.

'Surely you can take an hour off?' she implored.

'No, I'm sorry, I can't, I have far too much to do. You go, Patti, it's all right.' And yet the thought of Kiel taking her friend out, or any other girl for that matter, caused a tiny quiver of resentment.

As they went out through the doorway Patti turned and grinned and gave Tamara the thumbs-up sign. Tamara tried to smile back, but failed, and she could not help thinking that Kiel had made no effort to persuade her to join them.

She worked furiously and it was almost three when he returned. She heard him whistling as he strode along the corridor, and she held her breath, but he walked right past her door and into his own office, and she did not see him again for the rest of the day.

Nor did Patti phone her that evening, which she found surprising. She had expected her friend to tell her everything. The more she thought about it, the more strange it seemed. Perhaps they had felt a mutual attraction? Perhaps they were even out again together now?

Even as the thought occurred to her Tamara was dialling Patti's number, and when her friend did not answer she knew she had guessed correctly. And instead of feeling pleased for Patti she felt the green eye of jealousy gnawing away inside her. She tried to tell herself that she did not care, that she hated him and Patti was welcome to him, but it made not the slightest bit of difference.

The next morning Kiel called her into his office and she found herself looking closely at his face for any sign that he had a new love in his life. 'Is something wrong?' he asked, his eyes narrowed and distinctly chilly. 'Have I egg on my chin?'

Tamara assumed one of her haughtiest expressions. 'Of course not.'

'I'm relieved about that. So why are you looking at me as though you're trying to memorise my face? You're not thinking of packing in your job and leaving, are you?' A faint smile accompanied his words.

'You'd love that, wouldn't you?' she challenged, her very beautiful brown eyes shooting darts of hostility.

'It might make things easier,' he acceded. 'On the other hand, I would be losing an excellent designer.'

'I've no doubt you know plenty of other designers, the same as you do setters,' she thrust smartly. 'Is that what you're trying to do, Kiel—ease me out of here?'

'I wouldn't do that to Ben,' he said. 'He didn't make it a condition of his will, but I know that when he left me this company he expected me to keep you on for as long as you want.'

'And that's the only reason you're putting up with me, is it?' she flashed. 'In truth you hate the fact that you're forced to work with me almost as much as you hate me for causing your sister's death. It's a vicious circle, isn't it? But let me tell you it's not only me you're making unhappy, it's the whole workforce. And if Samantha Sheldon continues her mighty "I am" act you'll be getting a lot more complaints. I think you should tell her.'

By the time Tamara had finished there were two patches of high colour in her cheeks, her eyes sparking hostility, her whole body stiff with rejection.

'Sam doesn't take kindly to criticism,' he informed her tersely. 'And she's an exceptionally good setter, you're forgetting that.'

'You think that counts for more than happy workers?' she riposted. 'My father would turn in his grave if he knew what you were doing to his company.'

'What *I'm* doing?' He frowned harshly. 'Good lord, Tamara, Sam's been here one day, that's all. Aren't you over-reacting?'

'I can see what will happen.'

'I think you're wrong.' His grey eyes challenged her to disagree with him.

Her chin lifted. 'Time will tell. What did you want me for?'

For a long second he did not answer, their eyes locked together in a war of aggression. He wore a charcoal suit with a silver-grey shirt and a maroon tie. Usually he took his jacket off when he arrived, and rolled up his shirt sleeves, but not this morning. Perhaps he was going out, she thought hopefully. But she soon found out otherwise.

'I'm expecting Yves Delattre from Elegant in Paris. It could lead to some excellent business. I want you to be present. He's interested in a complete new range of gold and enamel jewellery. I understand that you studied enamelling in Japan?'

Tamara nodded. 'That's right, but I'm not sure that I'll have the time. I haven't even started on Princess Margherita's commission yet. It's all very well drumming up new business, but we can only do so much.'

His brows jagged together harshly. 'Are you saying that you cannot handle the extra work?'

'Not only me,' she snapped. 'All of us.'

'That's a defeatist attitude.'

Her eyes flashed angrily. 'Just because you work all the hours God made, it doesn't mean to say the rest of us have to do the same.'

'I'm not asking you to work over,' he told her crisply.

'So what are you expecting me to do, wave a magic wand?'

There was a moment's silence before he said, 'If it's getting too much for you I can employ another designer.'

Tamara was seething. 'What are you trying to do, make this into a multinational company? We have a reputation for being a caring, high-class jeweller. There are people who prefer the smaller company, who feel that they get better service that way. You're going to ruin all that if you expand.'

His eyes narrowed warningly. 'When I want your opinion I'll ask for it.'

Tamara eyed him for a long, silent moment, hating him yet feeling attracted to him at the same time. He was such a vitally masculine man that no woman could ignore his sensuality. But, damn him, she wouldn't give in to it. 'What time are you expecting Monsieur Delattre?' she asked flatly.

'Around ten.'

'I'll be here.' She strode towards the door, her chin high. He waited until her hand was on the knob and then he called her name. She turned and looked at him.

A faint smile curved his lips. 'Did I ever tell you how beautiful you are when you're angry?'

Tamara gritted her teeth and slammed the door, feeling even more angry when she heard his laughter, and she found it impossible to concentrate on her work after that. All she could see in her mind's eye was Kiel's smiling face. She jabbed her pencil down so hard on the paper that the point broke and she flung it across the room in disgust.

Just before ten she prepared herself for the meeting, combing her hair and sweeping the sides back with combs, otherwise leaving its long length to hang down to her waist. She was wearing a cherry-red woollen dress this morning with matching leather shoes, and the combs in her hair echoed the same colour.

At ten precisely Monsieur Delattre arrived and Tamara was duly summoned to Kiel's office. She had expected a dapper Frenchman; instead he looked more like a rugby player. He was easily as tall and broad as Kiel, about the same age, and with glossy black hair that fell forward across his brow. He had a scar down one cheek and wasn't terribly handsome, but his smile was warm when he shook her hand.

His English was perfect with only a faint trace of an accent. 'So you are the designer Kiel's been raving about?'

Tamara's brows rose as she slanted a questioning look at Kiel. He had been raving about her? She found that hard to believe.

'Yes,' went on Yves Delattre, 'he told me how brilliant you are, and that if anyone can interpret my ideas then you can. But he did not tell me how beautiful you are.'

'I shall do my best, naturally, Monsieur Delattre,' she said, flattered by his compliment, 'although I should warn you that I won't be able to start on them straight away.'

Kiel frowned harshly at her truthfulness, and she guessed he hadn't told this man how very busy they were.

'Of course, I understand,' said the other man at once, 'and please, call me Yves. Kiel and I are old friends—we were at Cambridge together. There's no need to be formal.' His blue eyes met and held hers for much longer than was necessary, and Tamara felt herself liking this man. After Kiel's abrasiveness it was nice to meet someone who treated her with courtesy and kindness.

The morning went quickly, with Yves outlining his ideas and Tamara pointing out anything that wasn't practical. When lunchtime arrived and Yves suggested she join them she accepted with a smile. This man was doing her good.

Kiel frowned abruptly. 'I don't think that would be a very good idea. Tamara normally has a working lunch.'

'Then it's time she had a change,' said Yves with a disarming smile.

Kiel shrugged his acceptance, though Tamara could see he wasn't happy. She guessed he was thinking about all the work she could be doing.

They ate at a Cantonese restaurant right in the Jewellery Quarter itself, and after finding out that she had no regular boyfriend Yves became even more attentive. His hand touched hers several times as he passed her different dishes, and more than once he commented on her beautiful hair.

Kiel's disapproval showed in his glacial eyes, though his tone was pleasant enough. If Tamara hadn't known better she would have said he were jealous. Presumably he did not approve of a prospective customer flirting with one of his employees.

She actually hated to think of herself as a simple staff member, and Kiel's attitude irritated her beyond measure. Consequently, when Yves asked her at the end of the meal if she would do the honour of joining him for dinner that evening, she immediately agreed. 'I'd love to, Yves,' she said with her widest and warmest smile.

'That is marvellous.' He took her elbow as they left the restaurant. 'I had no wish to spend an evening alone in a strange city. Perhaps you will show me the sights?'

'It will be my pleasure,' she said, feeling a sense of satisfaction as she caught a glimpse of Kiel's thunderous brow. What a balm to her wounded pride Yves was.

Outside Wilding Jewellery they parted company, Yves driving off in his hired car, after confirming their arrangements for that evening, while she and Kiel walked side by side into the building.

She waited for the censuring words that she knew would come, but was reprieved when Sam Sheldon called out to Kiel as they crossed the shop floor.

Tamara left him talking and went up to her office, though she could not help looking down at them. Why, she asked herself, was it one continual battle fighting off the attraction she felt for Kiel? If only he didn't hate her so; if only he could accept that Anna's death had been a tragic accident.

Samantha and Kiel stood together for ten minutes or more. The blonde girl was talking agitatedly and he seemed to be trying to soothe her. His hand rested on her shoulder for a long time and he brushed back a stray strand of hair from her face and Tamara quivered inside, hating herself for feeling any reaction, but unable to stop it.

When finally Kiel came upstairs he remained in his own office for over an hour before coming to see her. 'What was wrong with Sam?' she asked at once.

'Nothing was wrong, she was simply suggesting some improvements.'

'What a nerve!' Tamara's fine brows drew together angrily. 'I hope you told her to mind her own business?'

'Why should I?' he asked calmly. 'She's worked in several leading jewellery manufacturers in Europe so knows what she's talking about. She made some good points.'

'Is that why you brought her here?' she rasped. 'Will you be setting her up as your partner next? What is she to you, Kiel—your girlfriend? Your future wife?'

An eyebrow lifted. 'Do I detect a note of jealousy?'

'Like hell you do. She's welcome to you.' Tamara's brown eyes were as hard as pebbles, her whole body rejecting him. She felt close to tears. All her father had worked for was close to being ruined.

'I'm not here to discuss Sam,' said Kiel abruptly, and she noted he didn't deny a relationship with Samantha.

'I suppose you're going to tell me I shouldn't have accepted Yves' offer?' she spat.

Jutting brows rose, but his tone was calm. 'You can do better for yourself than him.'

Her chin lifted. 'Are you telling me who I should or should not go out with?'

'Yves asks out every girl he meets. He has quite a reputation, believe me, and it's not all good.'

Tamara nodded. 'I don't plan on going to bed with him, if that's what you're thinking. I just felt like a night out.'

'If that's what you want, why not let me take you?'

Her eyes widened. 'So that we can fight like cat and dog the whole evening? No, thank you.' But her heart skittered at the thought. Even now, here, in this room, she could not ignore his raw masculinity. Lord help her if they ever got friendly enough for a physical relationship. The very thought brought an ache to her groin and she turned away in case her feelings were mirrored in her eyes.

'Do you really not know what Yves expects of you?' His hands touched her shoulders and he spun her to face him.

Tamara looked into the depths of his eyes and felt herself drowning. What insanity it all was. 'I think I can handle myself,' she said tightly.

'You've had no experience of men like Yves.'

'If you knew what he was like, why did you insist that I meet him?'

His eyes narrowed. 'It was to be a business meeting, no more.'

'With you there to keep an eye on us? I wondered why you didn't approve when he asked me to join you for lunch.'

'Now you know, and I hope, Tamara, that you'll take my warning seriously.'

He still had not moved his hands, and Tamara could feel his warmth and his strength and her whole body ached. 'I have no intention of letting Yves try any funny business,' she said, her voice remarkably cool considering the hammer-beats of her heart.

'Good. Bear in mind that if you give him an inch he will take a mile. He has an insatiable desire for pretty girls.'

'Don't most men?' she scoffed.

'Not to the same degree,' he growled. 'And you, Tamara, are exceptionally beautiful. How can he resist you? How can any man?' He urged her to him and his hands slid behind her back until she was pressed so close that only their clothes separated them.

She could feel the strong beat of his heart and the heat of his skin, and she could smell his own particular brand of maleness, and although she wanted to push him away she could not.

It felt good to be held in his arms; it felt strangely right. They had known each other for so long that there was no awkwardness between them. It seemed like an inevitable part of their relationship.

When he lowered his head to kiss her, her own mouth came up to meet his and several long minutes passed before sanity asserted itself. Minutes in which he explored the moist softness of her mouth, in which their tongues touched and feelings ran high.

It was not until Tamara became conscious of the fact that they were in full view of the workshop that she pushed him savagely away. She dared not look down—it would be too embarrassing, especially if Samantha was watching. Instead she crossed the room and yanked her door open. 'Don't try that again,' she told Kiel crossly.

He gave a satisfied smile. 'I didn't notice you trying to stop me.' But it changed to a scowl as he added, 'A word of warning—don't respond like that to Yves unless you're prepared for the consequences.'

Tamara dressed with care for her evening out. She chose a full-skirted dress of emerald silk, with shoestring straps and a matching bolero. She swept her hair back with pearl combs and curled it into a cluster of ringlets. She widened her eyes even further with two complementary shades of grey eyeshadow, lengthened and thickened her lashes with mascara, and glossed her lips pale pink.

Around her throat she fastened a rope of emerald velvet, adorned with an emerald and pearl brooch that she had designed and made herself, fixing matching drop earrings to her ears.

When the doorbell rang she hastened to answer it, picking up her bag on the way. As her mother had now gone, Tamara had no intention of inviting Yves into the house. Not that she took Kiel's warning seriously, but this Frenchman was a stranger all the same.

'Good, you're ready,' he smiled, 'and may I say how ravishing you look?'

He looked good himself, she thought, in a grey-green safari-style suit, and when he took her hand and kissed it in a typically Gallic gesture she felt herself warming towards him.

They went to a nearby restaurant in Edgbaston where they ate home-made paté flavoured with almonds and Grand Marnier, and salmon steaks served in champagne sauce.

He was witty and entertaining, his eyes on her constantly, his legs touching hers beneath the table. He made no attempt to hide his interest and Tamara thought how nice it was to go out with a man who really appreciated her.

After their meal they drove around the city, Tamara pointing out the Bullring shopping centre, the town hall, and various other places of interest, and they finished up quite near to where she lived. 'I've had a lovely evening, thank you very much,' she said. 'But I'm tired now and I do have work in the morning. Would you mind taking me home?'

When he headed in the opposite direction she thought that he might be lost. 'Yves, Edgbaston's that way. If you turn down here you can head back.'

'The night is still young,' he said blithely, ignoring her instructions and continuing on into the city centre, showing her that he was not as ignorant of Birmingham as he had made out. 'Surely you don't begrudge me another hour of your charming company?'

Tamara realised she had no choice, but when he nosed into an underground car park beneath a hotel a feeling of unease settled in her stomach. 'Is this where you're staying?'

Yves smiled and nodded. 'Have another drink with me at least. I can't believe you're tired already.'

But when he ushered her into the lift instead of guiding her into one of the hotel's lounges she gave an inward groan. 'Yves, I don't think we should go to your room.'

'Why ever not?' He looked deeply affronted. 'Are you afraid of me? I promise, I don't bite.'

The smile that accompanied his words put Tamara at her ease. She was taking Kiel's warning too literally. And when he poured her a drink and they sat down, he in an armchair, she on an overstuffed couch, she began to relax. She had been worrying for nothing.

'Have you kept in touch with Kiel ever since you left Cambridge?' she asked.

Yves shrugged. 'Off and on.'

'You must have been in contact with him fairly recently to know that he now owns Wilding Jewellery.'

'Your late father's firm, I believe?' His eyes were sharp on her face.

'That's right.'

He frowned as he saw the shadow in her eyes. 'You're not happy that it now belongs to Kiel?'

It was Tamara's turn to shrug. 'I had expected to take over the running of it myself.'

'And so you should,' he said. 'Didn't your father believe in women in business?'

'He thought I was better placed as a designer.'

Yves rose from his chair and sat on the silk-covered seat beside her, taking her hand into his. 'For what it's worth, Tamara, you have my sympathies.' And when she did not immediately pull away from him he slid his arm about her shoulders and edged closer.

Tamara knew he was going to kiss her and she did not mind—he was the perfect antidote to Kiel—but she was not prepared for the fierceness of his kiss, or the ardour that was pulsing through him.

'Yves, please!' She tried to push him away, but he was resolute, his kiss deepening, his tongue forcing its way inside her mouth.

She rained her fists on his back and managed to break her mouth free. 'Yves, stop it, please stop it.'

'You don't want me to kiss you?' He looked hurt.

'Not like that. I really think I ought to go.' She attempted to stand but he pulled her back down again.

'Tamara, how can you do this to me? Did you not enjoy our evening?'

'Yes, of course, Yves, but——?'

'Then surely I deserve a little reward? I want us to be friends, Tamara, good friends. Kiel is a fool if he hasn't made you his own.'

'I don't want to belong to any man,' she protested, feeling alarmed now and wishing she hadn't let him bring her up to his room. His fingers were digging painfully into her shoulders and the scar on his face stood out lividly. 'Please, Yves, let me go.'

An unexpected loud knock on the door gave her the reprieve she needed. Taking advantage of the sudden relaxing of his hand, moving as swiftly as a hare in flight, she ran across to the door and snatched it open. Kiel burst into the room.

He took one look at her flushed face and dishevelled hair and guided her outside into the corridor. 'Wait for me,' he said harshly. The hotel door closed behind him and she could hear nothing, but when he came out he was smiling grimly. 'Let's go.'

His hand gripped her elbow as he punched the lift buttons, and as they made the descent there was an uncomfortable silence. Nor did he speak on the way home.

Outside her house he stopped the car and turned to her.

'I know what you're going to say,' she said at once, 'but I honestly never believed he would try to force himself on me.'

'In other words you thought I was making it up?'

Tamara shrugged. 'I don't know what I thought, but I felt sure I could handle him.'

'And what would have happened, do you think, if I hadn't come when I did?'

She shook her head. 'I'm hoping I would have been able to get through to him. In any case, what were you doing there?' she asked ungraciously.

His smile did not quite reach his eyes. 'I wondered when you'd get around to that.'

'Well?'

'What do you think I was doing?'

She shrugged. 'I suppose you wanted to see him about his order.'

'Like hell I did. I'd been sitting waiting for him to bring you back to his room. You're forgetting I know what he's like.'

'In which case,' said Tamara hotly, 'you took your time getting up there.'

'Is that all the thanks I'm going to get?'

'I don't believe you were coming to save me,' she said derisively. 'Why should you? You don't care a damn what happens to me.'

'Is that what you think?'

'It's what I've come to expect. Ever since Anna died you've either cold-shouldered me or taken pleasure in putting me down. If Daddy hadn't left you Wilding Jewellery we wouldn't even be seeing each other.'

'That's true,' he admitted.

'So you didn't have to be the hero and charge in to save my virtue.'

He eyed her coldly. 'I'll remember that another time when you're yelling for help.'

'There won't be another time,' she told him firmly. She would never be that stupid again. 'Thanks for the lift home—I'll see you in the morning.'

Tamara understandably had difficulty in sleeping, and her old nightmare became tangled up with Yves chasing her. The next day there were tell-tale shadows beneath her eyes that no amount of make-up could hide.

Kiel called her into his office halfway through the morning and he looked anything but happy. 'I thought I should tell you that Yves' order is cancelled.'

Faint colour rose in Tamara's cheeks. 'Oh, I'm sorry,' she said at once. 'I didn't realise he'd do that just because I stopped him making love to me. But it's not my fault, I——'

'Who's blaming you?'

She stopped short and stared at him. 'Isn't that why you want to see me?'

'I'm annoyed about losing the order, yes,' he admitted grimly. 'But Yves didn't cancel, I did.'

Tamara frowned. 'You told him you wouldn't go ahead—because of me?'

Kiel nodded.

Tamara did not know what to say. She swallowed a constricting lump in her throat. 'You didn't have to do that.'

'I don't want to do business with a man who treats my—my *employee*, so contemptuously.'

His emphasis on her status stung like a whip and Tamara's eyes flashed in cold dislike.

'Perhaps you'd like to tell me exactly why you did agree to go out with him?'

'I told you, I fancied a night out.'

'But with a total stranger, and after I'd warned you?'

'For the most part,' she told him defiantly, 'he was attentive and kind and amusing—a perfect gentleman in fact. I had a wonderful evening.'

'And you did it to make me angry?'

'Nothing of the sort,' she told him heatedly. 'I just thought it would be nice to go out with someone who wasn't continually harassing me.'

'You think I should forgive and forget the fact that you killed my sister?'

She gasped at the callousness of his words. 'Kiel, it wasn't my fault.'

'So you kept telling me, but it doesn't change my thoughts on the matter. Who would you prefer me to believe was at fault—Anna?'

Tamara closed her eyes in despair. Even to save her own face she could not tell him that his sister whom he idolised had indeed caused the accident. It was doubtful he would believe her anyway. He would think she was making it up to save her own face.

'I think you'd better go.'

She turned and, without looking at him again, left the room. One day, one day, if he pushed her too far, she would tell him exactly what his innocent little sister had been up to. And it was all his fault. He had thought he was so perfect, when in fact he had driven his sister to take drugs!

For the rest of the day Tamara found it difficult to concentrate. The incident with Yves and Anna's death became inextricably interwoven in her mind, and never had she been so glad when the hands on the clock reached five.

Yet even when she got home there was no respite. She had just finished eating her dinner when Patti turned up. 'You're not going out, are you?' she asked when she saw her friend's frown. 'I've not called at a bad time?'

'No, of course not, come in. I've had a hell of a day, that's all.' She led her friend into the plant-filled conservatory overlooking their large, landscaped garden and swimming-pool, covered at this time of year, but used frequently during the summer months.

'What's happened?' asked Patti, dropping down on one of the plump-cushioned cane chairs. 'Is it Kiel again?'

'Who else? Isn't it always him?'

Patti shook her head. 'I must confess I found him a perfect gentleman, although he's a bit of a woman-iser, isn't he? I saw him out with that new setter of yours the other night.'

'You did?' It was something Tamara had suspected but the proof filled her with despondence.

'I'm sorry to be the bearer of bad news,' said Patti ruefully. 'They were eating in the same restaurant and were so wrapped up in each other that he didn't even see me.'

Tamara was not surprised at that; what did surprise her was how deeply she was hurt. It shouldn't matter to her one jot what Kiel did in his spare time.

'So what's gone wrong this time?' asked Patti. 'You look truly awful.'

'Thanks a lot,' Tamara grimaced, 'but Kiel's not the whole cause of it.'

Patti's green eyes widened. 'Then who is?'

'I had a set-to with a customer—a friend of Kiel's actually. I went out with him last night and he came on a bit heavy.'

Patti grinned. 'Don't you see life?'

'It's not funny,' returned Tamara shortly.

'You look as though you came out of it in one piece. He didn't—you know...?'

'No, he did not. Kiel took it upon himself to play the guardian angel, though I didn't need him, and now we've lost the business and Kiel's blaming me for it.'

Patti's eyes widened but she said nothing.

'Well, not exactly, but it was implied. And the whole Anna thing was raked up again, and if you want to know I'm sick up to here of Kiel Kramer.' She held her hand up to her chin.

Patti took a deep breath and looked at her friend. 'I really don't know why you two keep rubbing each other up the wrong way. Why don't you both admit your attraction and let bygones be bygones?'

'Kiel, attracted to me? You must be joking. And he'll never let go of the fact that I caused Anna's death. He hates the sight of me.'

'And how do you feel about him?' asked Patti.

Tamara shrugged. 'I can't even understand this myself, but deep down I'm attracted to him. It's stupid, isn't it? Whenever he comes near me I find myself responding, even when we're fighting.'

'Is it any wonder?' said Patti. 'He's a hell of a guy. And he doesn't hate you. Do you know, when he took me out to lunch the other day he never stopped talking about you?'

'He didn't?' asked Tamara incredulously.

'No, he didn't. He sang your praises from the time we left the office until he dropped me off after we'd eaten.'

'I don't believe you.'

Patti shrugged. 'It's true. He told me how good you were at your job and how much faith he has in you. He said that he didn't think the firm would do so well if it weren't for your designs.'

'That doesn't mean he likes me on a personal level,' scoffed Tamara.

'I think he does,' said Patti softly. 'Why don't you let him see how you feel? Perhaps all he needs is some encouragement. It must be difficult for him now that he's actually your boss.'

'Don't you believe it,' said Tamara quickly. 'He loves the power it gives him. And I have my pride. No, thanks, Patti, I'll go on as I am. Besides, would he take you out again if he fancied me?'

Patti frowned. 'What do you mean?'

'Didn't you go out with him again on Monday night?'

'No.'

'But I rang and you weren't in. I thought that . . .'

Patti smiled mysteriously. 'Actually I did have a date. That's why I've come to see you. I want to tell you all about him.'

Kiel was forgotten as they discussed the new man in Patti's life—a friend of her brother who'd turned up out of the blue after living in the States for three years. It sounded as though it was serious.

When Patti finally stood up to leave she gave her friend a hug. 'Keep your chin up, Tammy, things are never as bad as they seem. One day I was bemoaning the fact that no one wanted me, and now here I am the happiest girl in the world. It could happen for you just as quickly—and I hope it's Kiel,' she added cheekily.

The rest of the week passed uneventfully, Kiel treating her with cool politeness, though she noticed that he spent more and more time talking to Samantha. The girl even came up to his office and spent long minutes shut away with him, and when that happened Tamara felt jealousy gnawing away inside her, because afterwards Samantha always had that look of a woman who had been well and truly kissed.

She spent the weekend shopping and gardening, and on Monday morning Carol came into her office with a letter. 'Kiel's not in this morning so I thought I ought to let you see this. We could be in big trouble.'

CHAPTER FOUR

TAMARA read the brief letter which came from a top jeweller's in London and frowned. It could be a genuine mistake, but she did not see how. She must have their stock of emeralds checked immediately to see if any more of them were synthetic, but if not it meant that someone had deliberately switched the stone when the ring had been set. And it didn't take much working out to know who had done it. The question was: why?

'I'll deal with this,' she said to Carol. 'You needn't say anything to Kiel.'

Tamara took the emeralds to a jeweller friend of hers who had the necessary laboratory equipment to check them, and he discovered to her surprise that all of their stock was synthetic. 'It looks as though someone's played a dirty trick on you.'

'You can say that again,' said Tamara grimly. And it put Samantha in the clear because she had only been issued with the necessary stones for the jobs she was working on. Tamara herself had the key to the safe in which their stock was kept.

This wasn't something she could handle alone. Kiel would need to contact their suppliers and apologise to their understandably irate customer. It certainly wouldn't bode well for future orders.

When he arrived after lunch she went straight into his office and placed the small bag of stones and the letter on his desk. 'I've had them checked, and they're all synthetic,' she said, when she had given him time to read it. 'I suspect our suppliers.'

'And what are you doing with this letter?' he barked, his eyes an icy grey. 'Why didn't it come straight to me?'

Tamara had expected his anger and was ready for it. 'Carol thought it needed handling promptly; that is the only reason.'

'And what gives you the right to go over my head?' He was not giving an inch.

'Heavens, Kiel, I don't see that it matters who's done the checking,' she retorted furiously. 'The fact of the matter is that someone's tried to swindle us, and we could lose a valuable customer because of it.'

He nodded grimly, reluctantly agreeing with her. 'Leave it with me.'

In other words, she was dismissed. When he called her back she was almost out of his office, and she stood in the doorway and waited to hear what he had to say.

He rose from his desk and walked towards her and Tamara felt the familiar awareness begin to build up. His mouth was still grim, but there was something else in his expression, something she could not quite work out. 'You look wan, Tamara. Are you all right?'

'Would you care if I wasn't?' she snapped.

'I'm not completely the cold-hearted brute you seem to think.'

You could have fooled me, thought Tamara, but she felt warmed that he had taken the trouble to ask, especially at a time like this. She gave a faint smile. 'I'm fine, thank you.'

'How are you coping with your mother away? I imagine looking after a house that size doesn't give you much leisure time?'

She lifted her shoulders and gave him a puzzled frown. 'I can't believe you're that interested.'

His nostrils flared angrily. 'I am almost one of the family, Tamara.'

'If you were you wouldn't treat me the way you do,' she retorted.

He sighed deeply and impatiently. 'Will you let me take you out to dinner tomorrow?'

Her eyes widened. This was the last thing she had expected. 'What will that solve?'

'Dammit, Tamara, you're a very beautiful and a very provocative lady.' He put his hands on her shoulders and urged her towards him.

She felt the immediate warmth of his body and his sexuality in that moment was overwhelming, but she would not let herself be swayed. 'Is that what you tell Samantha as well?' she asked coldly.

His eyes narrowed. 'What's Sam got to do with it?'

Tamara eyed him steadily, lifting her chin just a fraction. 'I know you took her out to dinner the other night.'

'You saw me?' His brows rose in surprise.

'No, but my friend Patti did, and I had a very good account of the way you were behaving.'

'It sounds as though your friend read more into it than there was.'

'I don't think so,' she retorted. 'I've seen the way she looks at you, the way you always stop and speak to her when you're down in the workshop, and she's beginning to spend a lot of time up here. It speaks for itself.'

His lips quirked. 'Does it worry you?'

Like hell! 'Not in the least,' she answered off-handedly, hoping she was a good enough actress to hide her jealousy.

'I think you're lying.'

'Why would I do that?'

'You tell me.'

'Let's say I don't think much of your taste. She looks to me like the type of girl who's only interested in a man's bank balance.'

'You're wrong there,' he told her firmly. 'I've known Samantha a long time, I know exactly what she's like. But she's not the point in question at this moment. Will you have dinner with me?'

'No,' she said abruptly, 'I'm too busy.'

'Then how about the weekend? Dinner on Saturday night? Or a drive to the coast on Sunday? Perhaps even both?' His hands moved from her shoulders to rest on her nape beneath the fullness of her hair; his thumbs sought the soft skin behind her ears.

Tamara's pulse-rate crept up and she found it impossible to look away. There was something hypnotic about Kiel in this mood. She found herself weakening. Perhaps she would go, just this once.

'I'll think about it,' she said, 'on condition that you don't drag up the past. If it's your intention to fill every minute blaming me for what happened to Anna, then forget it. I won't come out with you.'

A muscle jerked in his jaw but it was instantly controlled, and he slid his finger across her cheek until he was touching the corner of her mouth. 'I make no promises. When's it to be? Saturday or Sunday?'

Tamara felt an insane urge to touch his finger with her tongue, to press his hand to her face, to offer her mouth up to his. But she knew it was madness and she twisted away. 'Saturday night,' she replied, appalled to hear how breathless she sounded. A whole day would be far too much to handle.

'So be it.'

The week seemed to fly. The mystery remained as to how the synthetic emeralds had appeared, their suppliers promised to look into it, and an apology was duly made to their customer with the emeralds being replaced in the ring.

Tamara felt a strange excitement at the thought of going out with Kiel, and she didn't know why. It could turn out to be the biggest disaster of all time. In fact he was probably planning her humiliation.

She recalled his words on that day she had come back from Japan and found out he was her new boss. 'Have you any idea how I've suffered because of you?' 'It will give me the opportunity to get a little of my own back.' So far he had done nothing. Had he been waiting for her to relax and play into his hands? Was she doing just that?

After much deliberation she chose to wear a deceptively simple opera-topped, soft peach, satin-look silk dress that skimmed her curves and was delightfully feminine. Its matching jacket was embroidered delicately with seed-pearls. She wore no jewellery, except for a string of pearls which she twisted through her hair as she arranged it in a perfect chignon. The effect was stunning simplicity.

When Kiel turned up at two minutes to eight his eyes were riveted; he took in every tiny detail, even down to the fact that she was wearing very little underneath.

Tamara's skin warmed beneath his appraisal and she found it impossible to drag her eyes away from him, and she hoped she hadn't made a mistake in agreeing to go out this evening.

In contrast to her pastel shades he was wearing a dark navy lounge suit, with a white-collared grey and navy striped shirt. He looked as sartorially elegant as

always and, although Tamara hated to admit it, th.
made a handsome pair.

He helped her into his red Mercedes, which had the
rich smell of new leather, and she sank down on the
seat. In the few seconds it took him to walk round to
his side she had snapped on her seatbelt and tried to
mentally compose herself. It was hard when every
nerve-end responded to him, and she wished with all
her heart that she didn't feel this physical attraction.
It could destroy her.

He headed away from the city in a southerly
direction and Tamara was conscious of his every
move, his hand close to her as he changed gear, the
flexing of the muscles in his leg when he braked or
dipped the clutch. The whole car became filled with
his presence and she found herself clenching her hands
tightly in her lap in an effort to control her feelings.

It was not until they reached the Stratford road that
Tamara realised exactly where he was taking her. Her
heart fluttered anxiously. 'This is the way to your
house.'

'That's right,' he confirmed with a softly mocking
smile.

Tamara's nerves began to tighten. 'I don't want to
go there.'

'It's as good a place as any to eat. My housekeeper
is an excellent cook; you won't be disappointed.'

The thought of spending the entire evening alone
with him in his house filled her with—with what?
Horror? Excitement? Fear? Pleasure? A combination
of them all? 'I don't think it's a good idea.'

'My name's not Yves,' he thrust suddenly and savagely. 'Though lord knows I'm human enough to find
you attractive.'

d him! But it made no sense. 'I thought
d me?'

o, make no mistake about that. You took
aw... person I loved most in this world. I shall
never forget that, ever. But you're also a very beautiful and very provocative lady, and I can't forget that
either.'

'If you're suggesting what I think you are, then turn
round right now,' she told him tightly, her body
scorching at the thought. 'I have no wish to indulge
in any sort of sexual relationship.'

He gave a snort of anger. 'Grow up, Tamara. We're
all in charge of our own destiny. I have no intention
of forcing myself on you.'

At least that was something. Tamara's heart skittered along at an alarming rate and she was still apprehensive when they arrived at his house a quarter
of an hour later. She had been here often when Anna
had been alive, but this was the first time since.

It was a beautiful Tudor building on the outskirts
of Henley-in-Arden. Originally it had been his parents'
house, but he had liked it so much that he had stayed
on after they'd died, and he had a housekeeper and
gardener to look after things.

Welcoming lights lit up the front of the house, and
inside he ushered her into what she recalled had been
his parents' sitting-room. It was still furnished exactly
the same in beiges and rusts, and the deep, comfortable armchairs looked every inch as inviting.

He took her jacket, his fingers lingering on her
softly perfumed skin, and Tamara felt unbearable
pleasure despite her distrust. He had said he would
not force himself on her, but he had said nothing
about a slow seduction. She felt like a fly caught in

the innocuous-looking strands of a spider's web and she wished she knew what was going on in his mind.

She sat on the edge of one of the chairs, her ankles demurely crossed, knowing that she would need to constantly keep her wits about her if she wasn't to succumb to his overt sexuality.

'What will it be—gin, sherry, a glass of wine?' His grey eyes met hers, his earlier anger gone, warmth in his gaze, as there had been on the night of her mother's dinner party. For whose benefit was he putting it on this time?

'A small dry sherry, please,' she answered quietly.

'Taking no chances?' he mocked.

Tamara eyed him but said nothing, and when he gave her her drink she twisted the exquisite crystal between her fingers, observing how the amber liquid enhanced each of the precise cuts in the glass. 'I don't see the point in any of this.'

His eyes narrowed. 'You're determined to spoil the evening, aren't you?'

'I think you're up to something, though I don't know what. It's out of character for you to be nice to me.'

'Did you have any cause to complain about my treatment of you before Anna died?' His tone was a degree colder.

Tamara shrugged. 'You were like a brother, I suppose. Not exactly loving, but I could always rely on you.'

Kiel nodded and this time his tone was gruff when he spoke. 'I wanted to be more than a brother to you.'

Her eyes widened. This was news to her. 'Was that why you kissed me that day you came to see my father?' Once again her heartbeats accelerated.

'You looked so grown up.'

'And you frightened me to death.'

He paused in the act of sipping his drink and looked at her curiously. 'In what way did I frighten you?'

'You were so much older and wiser, so different from the boys I normally knocked around with.'

'None of them had kissed you like that?'

None of them had affected her as he had! Still did! She shook her head.

'And you still haven't grown up, have you? You're still running away from me.'

'You've made sure of that.'

A glint of anger darkened his eyes. 'Drink up and let's eat.'

His elderly housekeeper, Mrs Brookes, had cooked an excellent meal which she served in his elegant dining-room before discreetly disappearing.

And after dinner, when conversation had been kept to safe topics, they returned to their easy chairs in the sitting-room.

'I have your father to thank for getting me interested in jewellery in the first place,' Kiel said. 'When I was a boy he often took me into his workshop and showed me what was going on. How the moulds were made, the mounts, the setter's job, et cetera. I was intrigued, especially by all the different coloured stones, and I knew I wanted to join him when I grew up.'

'So this had all been arranged for a very long time?' accused Tamara with a sudden spurt of anger. Here was irrefutable proof that he had favoured this man all along. 'Did he think I wasn't good enough to run the company for him?' she asked in a choked voice.

'Definitely not. He knew you could run it easily— but who else could make such a good job of the de-signing? And there's no doubt about it, Tamara, you are excellent. It's a natural talent that you possess and it would be criminal to waste it.'

'Then why didn't he tell me that, instead of letting me go on thinking I would be his natural successor?'

Kiel shrugged. 'We will never know.'

She looked down at her glass, twisting it round and round in her fingers, her mouth tight, her thoughts chaotic. The next second his own hand closed over hers and feelings of a different kind chased through her.

He took her drink out of her hand and pulled her to her feet, and idiot that she was she let him. And when his mouth closed over hers there was only the slightest hesitation before she slid her hands behind him in complete surrender.

Her lips parted and she accepted his urgent kiss with a fierce wave of hunger, and when his hand moved to the softness of her breast she could not contain a tiny gasp of sheer pleasure. Her flesh hardened and swelled to this first, intimate touch.

She wore no bra beneath the thin silk of her dress and his thumb stroked in an intoxicating rhythm. She strained against him, feeling his arousal, feeling an excitement in her that threatened to spiral out of control.

When he slipped the thin straps from her shoulders Tamara's eyes never left his face, seeing the desire and the admiration as he exposed her breasts. 'Beautiful,' he breathed, 'quite beautiful.' Almost reverently he cupped them in his hands, and then his head lowered to take first one and then the other aching peak into his mouth.

A moan escaped the back of Tamara's throat; triggers of sensation ran right down between her breasts to her groin. She felt on fire and moved against him with unconscious sensuality, her fingers entangled in the wiriness of his hair. It was a moment of magic and—what was she doing responding to a man who hated her?

In sudden disgust she pushed him from her, her eyes flashing her anger. 'How dare you?'

To her astonishment he grinned. 'How dare I what? Kiss you? I didn't notice you trying to stop me. In fact I would go so far as to say that you were thoroughly enjoying it.'

'Damn you!' she rasped, fighting for breath, hating him for making her respond like this.

'Will you come out for the day with me tomorrow?'

His audacity stunned her. 'You must be joking!'

'I'm perfectly serious.'

And she was a fool, because her heart was telling her to accept while her head said it would be insanity. Despite his lovemaking she had enjoyed this evening—or because of it! She closed her eyes, still feeling his mouth on hers, her breasts still throbbing a response. What madness it all was.

'Tamara?' The taut, hard lines that seemed almost a permanent part of his face were relaxed. In this moment it was difficult to imagine the tough, uncompromising man who was making her life hell.

Perhaps he'd had a change of heart? Perhaps he realised that he had been too hard on her? Should she give him another chance? If they were friends it would certainly make life easier at the office.

He could see she was weakening. 'I'll pick you up at ten.'

To her disgust she felt herself nodding. She only hoped she wouldn't live to regret it. Kiel had a power of persuasion that she found truly remarkable.

When he suggested taking her home Tamara was astonished to discover it was after midnight. How could it be that late? Where had all the hours gone?

On the journey she laid her head back against the seat, her eyes closed, affecting tiredness. But in fact she was more wide awake than she had ever been, completely conscious of Kiel beside her, still feeling his hands on her body, still churning with sensation, her whole being attuned to his.

He stopped his car outside her house. 'Would you like me to come in with you?'

His tone was soft and encouraging but Tamara shook her head. 'I'll be fine, thank you.'

'Ben was always worried about how you'd cope on your own if anything happened to him and your mother.' Still there was that consideration in his voice.

Tamara smiled faintly. 'He didn't like to think I'd grown up. He always treated me as though I were a child.'

'He made me promise to look after you.'

She stiffened. 'He did what?' Everything suddenly fell into place. 'If the whole object of this exercise is for the sake of my father, then forget tomorrow.' And to think she had actually thought he was unbending towards her! 'I don't want to go out with you again— ever! Goodnight.' Feverishly she opened the door and scrambled out.

'Tamara, wait!' Kiel's voice was urgent. He was clearly startled by her reaction.

But she ignored him, racing up the steps, not stopping until she was safely inside. She half expected him to follow, waiting, listening, prepared to threaten him with the police, but instead she heard the sound of his car moving away.

She slowly climbed the stairs to her bedroom. Why hadn't she guessed? Why hadn't she known that her father would say something like that? Even so, Kiel's conscience must have been pricked for him to put himself out so much considering the way he felt about her. Well, he needn't bother again. She didn't need him; she didn't need any man.

Her father had let her down, he had let her down badly, but she would do her designing job, she would do it to the best of her ability, and she would stick it for as long as she could. Only if things got really unbearable would she leave, perhaps even start up on her own. Bill would come with her, she knew that, and probably Paul. She didn't have to stay and put up with Kiel's insults.

On Sunday morning, after she had eaten a simple breakfast of coffee and toast, Tamara left the house. It was a cold, crisp day, exactly right for blowing away the cobwebs—and thoughts of Kiel Kramer! Damn him, he had kept her awake most of the night, and what little sleep she did have had been tortured by nightmares.

Birmingham Botanical Gardens were only a short distance away and it had been years since she'd visited them. They wouldn't be very busy at this time of year. Solitude was just what she needed.

But she had not realised that the gardens did not open until ten on a Sunday, and while she was waiting she felt a touch on her arm. 'I thought we had a date?'

She swung around, her eyes wide, her pulse skidding at the sight of Kiel. 'And I thought I'd made it plain I didn't want to see you.' It was difficult keeping her tone hard when her body was betraying her.

'So why are you hiding here if you thought I wouldn't come?' He wore straw-coloured trousers and a brown leather jacket over a thick Aran sweater. He looked more rawly masculine than ever. But gone was the relaxed and sensuous man of the night before. His mouth was compressed into the hard, thin line that she knew so well, his eyes flintlike, making no effort to hide his anger.

'I'm not hiding,' she retorted defensively. 'I needed some air and this seemed the ideal spot to walk. How did you find me?' Her jeans were tucked into black leather boots and her hands pushed deep into the pockets of a red quilted jacket. The keen wind had brought colour to her cheeks, disguising the true pallor of her skin.

'I followed you.' He made the announcement with grim pleasure. 'I had a feeling you'd try to run away.'

At that moment the doors were opened and the tiny gathering of people surged forward. Tamara moved with them, deliberately turned her back on Kiel, missing his harsh frown.

'I've come to take you out as planned,' he rasped. 'Don't say you're still going in there?'

'It wouldn't work, my coming with you,' she said over her shoulder. 'Not now I know why you're doing it. Why don't you leave me alone?'

'Because I damn well don't want to,' he snarled, and she could feel his breath hot on her cheek. 'Tell me what you're afraid of, Tamara.'

They had reached the desk and she slid her money beneath the glass window, taking her ticket and moving quickly away. 'Nothing at all,' she answered coolly.

Kiel swore and dug in his pocket for a couple of coins, following her into the glasshouses where an endless variety of tropical plants grew in heated profusion. 'This is ridiculous,' he growled as he caught her up.

'I don't think so.'

'But last night——'

'Last night I made a mistake,' she said sharply.

'Last night you let the true you show through.'

'And made a fool of myself,' she hissed. 'Do you really think I'm that gullible I don't know what you're after?'

He frowned and spun her to face him.

'Let me go,' she cried, tearing herself away and brushing past a couple who were admiring a particularly fine orange tree.

He caught her up outside and, when she could see there was no sense in fleeing any more, her footsteps slowed. He fell into step beside her. 'Would you mind telling me what you're talking about?' he asked roughly.

'Didn't I make myself clear?' she snapped. 'I know it was my father's dearest wish that we get our act together, but I don't think he meant for you to take things this far. You're depraved.'

He snorted derisively. 'Hell, Tamara, your father has nothing to do with this. You've convinced me that you don't need anyone to keep an eye on you.'

'Then why insist that I spend the day with you?' Why torment her like this?

He didn't answer. Instead he said roughly, 'Anna used to like it here, you know. I brought her a lot just after our parents died.' He stood a moment and looked around, as though still seeing Anna as a young girl running and skipping across the wide expanses of grass, playing hide and seek in the trees. 'We had lots of fun together.'

They had been extraordinarily close, Tamara knew that, drawn together by the death of their parents. And there was nothing she could say to him now; she was the one who had taken his sister from him.

The memory of that day was always painful when it returned and she walked away from Kiel, swallowing hard, fighting back tears. She had loved Anna too. Didn't he ever think of that?

He caught her up, his face all harsh lines and angles. 'Why the hell didn't you drive with more care?'

'For pity's sake, Kiel, it was an accident. I couldn't do a thing about it.'

'I still don't see how you swerved off the road. You must have been drinking.'

'I wasn't, and I was breathalysed to prove it, as you know very well. It was a wet night, I skidded.'

'You were driving too fast.'

'Kiel, we've been through all this once. Why are you torturing yourself? Talking about Anna like that won't——'

'Won't bring her back? Is that what you were going to say?' he cut in coldly. 'I don't know why you took her to that damn party in the first place. There were kids there taking drugs, did you know that?'

He saw the shock on her face. 'No, I didn't think you would. You're too blind and stupid to see what's going on beneath your very nose. But what if she'd been persuaded to experiment? What then? Would you still be saying it wasn't your fault?'

Tamara closed her eyes. It would kill him if he knew that his darling little sister had already been into the drug scene.

'Look at me, damn you!' His fingers bit into her shoulders and he shook her savagely. 'To my dying day I'll hold you responsible for Anna's death. If there had been some way I could prove you were guilty of careless driving I'd have had you dragged through the courts on a manslaughter charge. As it is I have to mete out my own punishment.'

'The first step of which was to persuade my father to make his will out in your favour?'

'Dammit, Tamara,' he snarled, 'that's unfair. This is personal, between you and me, a bitter battle that will be fought for the rest of our lives. I hate you but, heaven only knows why, I find myself attracted to you as well. Isn't that rich? You've got beneath my skin like no one else ever has and I need and want you, and I intend having you.'

Tamara looked at the glitter in his eyes and felt afraid. A little bit excited too, but there was more fear than anything else. He sounded as though he meant business, as though, if she goaded him enough, he would take her in anger, despite assuring her that he never used force. It was a delicate situation. What could she say that would not add fuel to his fire?

'The fact that you also find me attractive helps,' he added firmly.

'No!' Wildly she shook her head. She must never let him think that. 'No, I don't. You're mistaken.'

'Am I?' he snarled. 'Why waste your breath denying it? Admittedly there's no love lost between us, but we're both physically attracted, and making love in those circumstances should be an exciting affair.'

'You sound as though you're planning rape,' accused Tamara, her breasts rising and falling as she fought for control.

'Not rape, my shocked friend. When I make love to you you'll be ready, have no doubts about that.'

They heard voices getting nearer and he dropped his hand to her elbow and urged her forward away from them, and her heart felt like a sledge-hammer in her breast. The thought of Kiel making love to her was indeed truly exciting, but she did not want him to do it in anger or revenge. If he tried that she would fight him every inch of the way.

She pulled savagely out of his grasp. 'I'll never be ready, Kiel. I hate you even touching me. Haven't you any idea at all how I feel?'

'Oh, yes, I know.' He grinned. 'I know exactly how you feel. I can almost see the shivers of pleasure that sensitise your skin, and your mouth opens in the most delightful way, your little pink tongue touching your lips, and your eyes—well, they're the most expressive eyes I've ever seen. They hide nothing from me, Tamara. They tell me everything. In fact, I doubt if any other man has ever affected you the way I do. Your capitulation shouldn't take long.'

Appalled that she had given so much away, Tamara was robbed of speech. It was true, everything he'd said was true, but she hadn't been aware that he knew it. Was she really so transparent? Could he tell simply by looking at her face what she was feeling and thinking?

She turned abruptly away and pretended an interest in the exotic birds in the aviary in front of them.

'Have you nothing to say?' he asked, tilting her chin with a firm finger and forcing her to look at him. His lips curved in a mocking smile, as if he knew exactly the confused state of her mind.

'I think I hate you.'

'A powerful emotion, and I know what I'm talking about. But it's also reputed to be akin to love. Do you believe that, Tamara?'

'No, I don't,' she crisped. And yet, deep inside, she was conscious of feelings other than hatred. A need for this man on different terms, a uniting of their bodies but not in anger. 'I think we're in a stalemate situation.'

'You prefer to deny the feelings of your body?'

'When the man in question is you, yes, I do,' she said heatedly. 'When I let a man make love to me it will be because I respect and love him.' She glanced at her watch and was amazed to see how long they had been walking.

'I think a cup of coffee and a bite to eat in the tea room would be a good idea,' said Kiel, following her line of thought.

'Personally, I was thinking of going home,' she told him coldly.

'To an empty house?' A brow rose sceptically. 'If you don't fancy it here we could find a restaurant— or even go back to my place?'

'No, thank you,' said Tamara shortly, memories of last night still too vivid in her mind. 'I'll settle for here.'

'I thought you might.'

His mocking smile irritated her and she stormed ahead. In the light and airy tea room he was consistently cheerful, and Tamara grew more and more distant. Now that she knew what she was up against it was her only defence. But it was hard when her body responded to him against her will, when every fibre of her being was constantly attuned to his sexuality. What was it about him that made her wish things were different between them?

And the more she thought about him, the more annoyed she became. Why couldn't she control her feelings? In a sudden surge of anger, not caring what Kiel thought, she pushed herself to her feet and marched out of the tea room.

Kiel swore, and, slapping a few notes on the table, followed. When he caught up with her he spun her to face him. 'What the hell's going on? What have I said or done this time?'

'Let's just say I don't want anything more to do with you,' she snapped. 'And will you let go my arm? You're hurting.'

'I'll do more than damned hurt,' he grated. 'Didn't I make myself clear what the position between us was going to be?'

'You lay one finger on me, Kiel Kramer,' she yelled, 'and I'll scream rape. You're worse than Yves, do you know that?'

His eyes hardened at her insult and he released her with a savage gesture that sent her stumbling to her knees on the grass. She looked up at him with hatred blazing in her face. 'Get out of my sight, Kiel Kramer.'

For a brief moment he held her gaze and Tamara felt the full impact of his contempt. Then he swung on his heel and headed for the exit. She was left to pick herself up.

CHAPTER FIVE

TAMARA'S nerves were knotted when she arrived at work on Monday morning, and it wasn't helped by the fact that she had a throbbing headache. Thinking about her disastrous meeting with Kiel had kept her awake most of the night, and her stomach contorted at the thought of facing him again. But she worried in vain—Carol told her that he was spending the day in London.

She took some aspirin but they did little to alleviate the pain in her head, and halfway through the afternoon she decided to call it a day. She was in the act of picking up her bag when Samantha marched unceremoniously into her office. 'I want to talk to you.'

Shocked by the girl's high-handed manner, Tamara said sharply, 'If it's to do with your job, then Kiel's the person to see.'

'It has nothing to do with work,' said Samantha, her chin high, her eyes scornful. 'Though I could make plenty of complaints if I wanted to—about the way some people treat me. But I'm not here to complain about anyone else. It's you.'

'Me?' Tamara's velvet-brown eyes widened. She couldn't imagine what the girl had got to say to her.

'Yes—you and Kiel, to be precise,' went on Samantha quickly. 'I want to know what's going on between you. Perhaps you weren't aware of the fact that he and I are old friends? More than friends, in fact.'

'Oh, yes, I know,' said Tamara evenly. 'You've made it pretty obvious to everyone here that you regard him as your personal property.'

'That's right,' spat the blonde girl. 'So what were you doing out with him yesterday? From what I hear you were not exactly acting like business colleagues.'

'And what did you hear?' asked Tamara icily, wondering at the same time who had seen them. She had been so worked up that she hadn't looked at any of the other people walking through the gardens.

Samantha's eyes were glacial. 'That you were holding hands, that he was very attentive to you, that you looked for all the world like lovers.'

The girl's possessive attitude incensed Tamara and she had a sudden unreasonable urge to put her in her place. 'I think my relationship with Kiel goes back much further than yours.' She accompanied her words with a smile. 'I've known him all my life, as a matter of fact. Has he told you that?' She could see by the girl's expression that he hadn't. 'I think you should be the one who leaves him alone.'

Samantha's deep blue eyes hardened. 'You think that just because your father once owned this company it gives you the right to tell everyone else what to do, don't you? Well, it doesn't. We're equals, you and I, and I want Kiel and I'm going to have him.'

'Would it have anything to do with the fact that he now has a company of his own?' asked Tamara coldly. 'Does that make him a more attractive proposition? Is that why you followed him here? Is that why you're putting the pressure on?'

Tamara knew that her intuition was right when she saw the defensive expression on Samantha's face, but it was gone in an instant and the girl looked at her scornfully. 'I love him.'

'But does Kiel love you?' asked Tamara coolly, her chin tilted. 'I think you should ask yourself that question.' She tucked her bag more firmly under her arm. 'Is that all? You're holding me up, in case you didn't know. I was just about to leave.'

'Where is he now?' snapped Samantha.

Tamara shook her head. 'I've no idea.'

The girl looked disbelieving, but she said crossly, 'Never mind, he'll phone me tonight. Or he'll simply turn up and we'll have an intimate supper for two. It won't be the first time.'

She walked out of the room and Tamara marched angrily down to her car, but it was a few minutes before she started the engine. She was disgusted with herself for feeling jealous. Why did it matter that Kiel was interested in Samantha? Why did it hurt so much? She preferred not to work out the answer.

At length she turned the key, but instead of easing her car out as normal she slammed her foot down on the accelerator. Then she had to stand on her brakes in order to avoid a head-on collision with Kiel just entering the car park. Even so, their bumpers met and crunched.

This was the last straw and Tamara jumped out of the car, her eyes blazing and her head pounding. 'What the hell do you think you're doing, driving in here at that maniacal speed?'

'I beg your pardon?' Kiel slowly hauled himself out and towered his height above her. 'It is I who should be asking that same question.'

'I thought you were in London.' Tamara did not realise she was admitting negligence.

'Well, I'm not, I'm here, and look what you've done to my car.'

'What *I've* done?' she yelled.

'It certainly wasn't my fault,' he roared back. 'You came tearing out as though all the hounds in hell were after you, and then you have the nerve to accuse me.' There was raw anger in his eyes. 'Where were you going in such a hurry?'

'Home,' snapped Tamara.

He shot a glance at his watch. 'At this hour?'

'I don't suppose it bothers you, but I happen to have a grinding headache.'

Immediately his face changed, his tone softened fractionally. 'I'll run you home.'

'No, thanks.'

'Have you taken anything for it?'

'Some aspirin.'

'Go and take something stronger and lie down. I'll come and see you this evening.'

'I wouldn't do that if I were you,' she said with a saccharin-sweet smile. 'Your girlfriend's expecting you.'

'Girlfriend?' He jerked, a frown stabbing his brow.

'Sam. She's been on a manhunt after you.'

His lips pursed. 'Did she say what she wanted?'

'I think that's for you to find out.'

'Which I'll do in a few minutes' time. I'll see you tonight,' he said firmly, getting back into his car and reversing out of her way.

Tamara did not look at him as she manoeuvred out of the car park and headed towards home. Once indoors she swallowed some tablets and went to bed, falling immediately asleep. The next thing she knew someone was touching her shoulder.

She opened her eyes with difficulty and met Kiel's cool grey gaze. Immediately she sat up in alarm, pulling the sheet up to her chin. 'What the hell are you doing here? Get out!'

'How's your head?'

'My head's all right, but you've no right forcing
your way into my house.' Her heart had begun a drum
tattoo within her breast. She felt far too vulnerable,
so very much aware of him as a desirable male animal.

'I did not force my way in,' he told her calmly. 'I
have a key. I've always had one, as you must know.
I rang the bell and I knocked on the door and there
was no answer. I was worried about you.'

'I bet,' snapped Tamara. 'You should have known
I'd be asleep. *Get out!*'

'I said I would come.'

'But not until this evening.'

'It is evening.'

Tamara frowned and glanced at her bedside clock.
He was right; it was half-past six. Had she really slept
all those hours? 'It's still wrong of you to come up
to my bedroom.'

'What are you scared of?' There was mockery in
his eyes now.

'You should know, after the threats you made.' And
she was as scared as hell that if he tried anything she
wouldn't be able to stop him.

His lips quirked. 'I'm still too much of a gentleman
to take advantage of a situation like this.'

'What a relief,' announced Tamara with deliberate,
heavy sarcasm, hoping he wouldn't realise that she
actually meant the words. 'Did you see Samantha?'

He nodded. 'She told me she had quite an
interesting conversation with you.'

Tamara's eyes flashed. 'And did she tell you what
it was about?'

He shook his head.

'No, I didn't think she would.'

'Perhaps you'd like to tell me?' A caustic smile accompanied his words.

'No, thanks. Most of it was far too personal to repeat. All I will say is that I don't think very much of your choice of friend.'

'Sam's doing a good job.' He frowned.

'And still upsetting everyone else into the bargain. You must know what she's like. Does having your lover close to you mean more than having happy employees? Can't you bear to be parted for those eight or nine hours a day?'

His eyes narrowed in anger and he stalked across to the door. 'I think I should go.'

Intimate supper for two! Tamara could not get the words out of her head. It was probably why he had come here so early. 'Are you having supper with her?' she asked bitterly, the words out before she could stop them.

'Would it bother you?'

'Not in the slightest.'

'Why is it I don't believe you?' He walked slowly back. 'I think it bothers you very much.' He bent low and pressed an unexpected kiss to her forehead. 'Why, Tamara, you're trembling.'

'With anger,' she cried. 'You're insufferable. Get out before I scream.'

'Would you really do that?' He looked amused by her erratic behaviour.

'Yes, I would,' she spat.

'But there's no one to hear.'

'We do have neighbours,' she told him caustically.

'In that case I shall have to stop you,' and his mouth was on hers almost before he had finished speaking.

Tamara could not ignore the undisguised pleasure that ran through her. Even her anger and her hatred paled beside this much stronger emotion. It was a situation she should have avoided at all costs.

The tension eased out of her body as his kiss deepened, every nerve in her responding, and she kissed him back with breathless hunger. She reached up and slid her arms around him—and the sheets slipped away—and she remembered too late that she was naked! She struggled then to free herself but Kiel held her firmly, allowing one hand to trail with indecent haste over her proud, firm breasts.

She closed her eyes, not wanting to see what he was doing, but the feelings he generated could not be brushed aside. Her adrenalin pumped and her whole body felt on fire.

'Proof indeed that I can take you any time I want,' he muttered harshly against her mouth.

The spell was broken. Tamara struggled to push him away. 'You swine!'

He laughed into her flashing eyes. 'It will only be a matter of time, Tamara, before you realise that you're fighting the inevitable.' With exaggerated care he pulled the sheets back over her. 'Goodbye for now, my sweet. I'll see you tomorrow.'

Tamara lay back and closed her eyes, annoyed that she had given herself away so easily, yet at the same time exulting in the feelings Kiel had aroused. Her body was still warm and tingling, and she touched her breasts with her hands, where his had been earlier, and she tried to imagine what it would be like to be friends with Kiel, to have a normal, loving relationship. It sounded like heaven, but it was the one thing she knew would never happen, and it was pointless thinking about it.

Several minutes went by before she found the strength to get up. Her headache, which had gone,

was threatening to return. She pulled on a warm
tracksuit and an anorak and let herself out of the
house. Perhaps some fresh air would clear her mind.
It was incredible the way she responded to Kiel when
every sane thought told her it was wrong. She was
playing right into his hands.

She walked and walked and eventually found herself
near Patti's house. On an impulse she knocked at the
door. It was opened by a young man she had never
seen before. He was of a similar build to Kiel, but his
hair was a much lighter brown and he had a cheerful
face.

'Who is it, Rory?' Patti's voice came from the
depths of the house.

'A beautiful young lady with gorgeous, long black
hair. I hope she's a friend of yours.' His eyes were
frankly admiring.

Patti appeared with a welcoming smile. 'Tammy,
how nice. Come on in. This is Rory—remember I told
you about him? And this, Rory, is my very best friend,
Tamara Wilding.'

Patti's house was small but homely, and they all
filed into her pine and willow pattern kitchen. 'I'll
put the kettle on. This is a rare honour, Tammy. What
have I done to deserve this visit?'

'I was out walking and——'

'Walking? You?' echoed Patti incredulously. 'I
don't believe it. What's happened to your car?'

'I needed some fresh air.'

'Come to think about it, you do look a bit peaky.
Is that man working you too hard?' And to Rory,
'Her boss is the answer to every woman's dream, but
they're determined to hate each other. It's crazy.'

'He must be crazy if he hates a good-looking girl
like you,' said Rory. 'He must be totally out of his

mind. How can he resist you? No wonder Patti's made sure we've never met.'

'Rory!' said Patti warningly.

He grinned and put his arm around her. 'It's all right, I prefer blondes, but you must admit your friend's a stunner.'

'So what exactly is wrong?' asked Patti, shrugging free and filling the kettle.

'Everything.' She could hardly tell her friend in front of Rory that she was bothered by her response to Kiel's kisses. In the past they had told each other most things and any problems had soon been sorted out, but if Patti was serious about Rory those days had come to an end. He looked so much at home she suspected he might have moved in.

Patti leaned back against the sink as she waited for the kettle. 'What do you mean, everything?'

'Oh, you know what he's like. I find it impossible to work with him, but what can I do about it? I'm even thinking about giving it all up.'

'It's as bad as that?'

Tamara nodded.

'Rory, I've run out of milk,' said Patti at once. 'Be a darling and go and get me a bottle.'

'But there's——'

'Rory!'

He looked from one to the other and grinned. 'I see, girls' talk. You want me out of the way? I'll go for a pint, but it certainly won't be milk.'

'Now,' said Patti the instant he had left the house. 'What's bothering you?'

'Can you hate a man and want him to make love to you at the same time?'

Patti's brows rose. 'It doesn't sound like hatred to me.'

'Well, maybe it's not exactly. I am attracted to him, I suppose, but I don't want to be—I don't want to even like him. Especially as he's still got it in for me for causing his sister's death. He brought it up again only yesterday.'

'Yesterday? Sunday? You saw him then?' Patti's eyes widened with curiosity and disbelief.

Tamara grimaced and nodded. 'I had a meal at his house on Saturday and I was going to see him again on Sunday, then we had a row, but he turned up anyway.'

'He sounds keen.'

'Keen to hurt me. He's so bitter, Patti, he's really taking it out on me.'

'Are you sure?'

'Of course I'm sure. Besides, there's Sam. You remember me telling you about her—Samantha Sheldon? She told me she has every intention of having Kiel—and I believe her. She's a very determined lady.'

'Does Kiel love her?' Patti frowned, obviously finding the whole story hard to believe.

Tamara shrugged. 'Who's to say? But he's having a meal at her house tonight.'

'And you feel as sick as a pig about it?'

'Yes,' she admitted reluctantly. 'I don't know what he sees in her. She's a bitch. We had a set-to at work today and I saw her in her true colours.'

'I still think you should let him see how you feel.'

'That's why I went out with him on Saturday,' said Tamara. 'I was taking your advice. But it didn't work out. Whenever we're together he reminds me about Anna. He'll never forgive me, ever.'

'Someone should tell him,' said Patti determinedly, 'that he can't go on blaming you for the rest of your life. Heavens, it was bad enough for you when it happened. Why should you have to go on suffering?'

'Because I took away all the family he had.'

'The man's insane.' Patti shook her head in exasperation. 'He needs to see a psychiatrist.'

Tamara could not help laughing. 'I doubt he'd be pleased to hear you say that.'

'But you're my best friend and I love you and I don't like to see you unhappy.'

'I'll survive.'

'Shall I have a word with him?' asked Patti gently. 'We got on pretty well together that time he took me out. I think he'll listen.'

'Don't you dare,' said Tamara at once. 'You'd only make matters worse. Heavens, he'd think I'd been telling tales.'

'Would it help if this Samantha woman were out of the way? Perhaps I ought to work on her?'

Tamara smilingly shook her head. 'Oh, Patti, I love you for trying to help, but it's my problem. I just needed to talk. And here's Rory back. I'll go now.'

They were so busy for the next few days that neither Tamara nor Kiel had time for private conversation. She did not fail to notice, however, that he seemed to find time for Samantha. There was no change there. Every time he walked through the workshop he would say something to her, or she would come up to his office, and in the end Tamara had to stop herself from looking out of her window. She noticed that Paul was watching them too.

She wished her father were still alive. There had never been any discontent among their workers then.

On her walk to Patti's on Monday evening Tamara had stopped to look at one of the church windows and was unable to get out of her mind the different shapes, from the Gothic arch of the window itself to all the varying sizes and contours of the coloured glass.

Blessed with an almost photographic memory, she drew what she had seen and picked out various details and reproduced them from many angles until finally she had what she was looking for. She knew now exactly what style she was going to use for Princess Margherita's necklace and earrings.

So engrossed was she in her sketches that she didn't hear Kiel enter the room. 'They're good, very good.'

His words startled her and a thousand tiny goose-bumps lifted on her skin.

'Vaguely Gothic, but not unless you know it's there. It's inspirational. Princess Margherita will love it. Where did you get the idea from?'

Tamara shrugged. 'Like most others I find my source and it grows. A church window gave me this idea.'

'It's brilliant. When will your sketches be finished?'

'In a few days.' She wished he would not stand quite so close. All her senses sprang into action. She could feel the overpowering warmth of him, smell the faint, lingering odour of his Givenchy aftershave, almost taste him.

'Perfect. She's shortly coming on a private visit to London. I'll fix a meeting and I'd like you to attend.'

'Me?' squeaked Tamara.

'Yes, you,' he mocked. 'This is extremely important. Princess Margherita might want to make some changes, though I doubt it. This is absolutely incredible. Diamonds and French blue sapphires are among her favourite stones.'

Tamara shot him a sharp glance. 'You knew that, and yet you let me find out for myself. Were you testing me?'

He shrugged. 'Maybe.'

'Well, thanks for nothing. I have all the time in the world for things like that.'

'Do you know how beautiful your eyes are when you're angry? It's one of the things that attracts me to you.'

'I don't want to know,' she snapped.

'They're like smoky quartz, and so wide and deep I feel I could jump inside and drown myself.'

'You're being very poetic all of a sudden,' she scorned.

'Perhaps that's how you make me feel.'

Her eyes flashed yet again. 'Now I know you're joking. I know exactly how you feel about me, and there's nothing sentimental about it. But if you think you can use me and play about with Samantha at the same time you can think again.'

'Play about with Sam?' His lips quirked as he tried to control a smile. 'What an absurd idea.'

'So you're serious about her. That's fine—so long as you keep your dirty paws off me!'

A muscle worked in his jaw which should have warned her. 'I think we ought to forget about Sam; she really doesn't enter into it.'

'How can you say that,' she demanded, 'when every single time you go downstairs you stop and talk to her?'

'Correction. She talks to me.'

'It's the same thing.'

'No, it isn't,' he assured her. 'But I can't ignore the girl, can I? And usually it's some query to do with her work.'

'Oh, yes? Am I expected to believe that when she's supposedly so expert at her job?'

Kiel's jaw tightened as anger began to replace his good humour. 'You never lose an opportunity to run her down, do you?'

'Not when she's disrupting the workforce.'

He snorted his disgust. 'One man alone doesn't like her.'

'One man has the guts to speak up,' she snapped. 'The rest tolerate her, but I don't know for how long.'

'You know that for a fact?'

'I use my eyes. This was such a happy place before you took over. Now it's a picture of gloom and doom.'

He looked down out of her window at the workshop. Everyone was busy, which was as it should be. But in the past there had always been jokes flying backwards and forwards—the men had been happy in their work. Now, one woman, one single, beautiful female, who should have been a fillip for their ego, had effectively demoralised them.

But Tamara did not expect Kiel to understand that. He saw no further than Samantha. Why did men always make idiots of themselves over women? Even as he watched, Samantha looked up and waved. He lifted his hand in a return gesture then turned back to Tamara.

'I see nothing wrong.'

'I knew you wouldn't. That woman's blinded your vision. Excuse me, I want to get on with this sketch.'

He said no more, but he stood and watched over her shoulder until Tamara felt ready to scream.

'I have tickets for the theatre tomorrow night. I'd like you to come with me.'

Her hand stilled. 'Are you sure you're asking the right girl?'

'Very sure,' he said softly, and his mouth came down until she felt his warm breath behind her ear. 'Very, very sure.'

Every one of her senses came into play and she longed to turn into his arms and say yes. But what foolishness that would be. He was still playing some kind of cat-and-mouse game with her. 'I'm sorry,' she said icily, 'I don't think it would be a good idea. Now will you please go, or I shall never get this finished?'

To her amazement he walked across to the door, but there was a mocking smile on his face when he looked back at her. 'You'll come, Tamara.'

The sketches were finished. Tamara looked at them with pleasure. Yes, she was very pleased with the outcome. In fact she thought it her best design ever. She picked them up and made her way to Kiel's office.

He called her in but did not look up when she entered. He was frowning in sheer disbelief at a piece of paper in his hand. 'Is something wrong?' she asked.

'I don't know—read this.' He thrust the letter at her.

Tamara quickly scanned the contents and immediately her happiness was spoilt. In fact she felt quite sick. 'I can't believe this has happened again. There has to be some mistake.'

'I intend getting to the bottom of it,' he crisped, standing up. 'Are those the sketches? Leave them on my desk.' He had gone before she could say any more.

Not emeralds this time, but pearls. A necklace especially commissioned by Lord Acton for his wife using only the very finest natural pearls set in a uniquely designed gold pendant. A lot of time had been spent on locating pearls as near spherical as possible and now their client, through his solicitor, was claiming that cultured ones had been used instead. Unless there was some very good explanation they would be sued for fraud.

Tamara was horrified. In all their years of trading they had experienced nothing like this. They had one of the highest reputations among jewellery manufacturers—and now their name was being tarnished!

She stood at Kiel's office window watching as he talked to the men. Heads were being shaken, and when he came back he said, 'No one knows anything about it. Ask Carol to let me know who supplied them.'

'It was Briggs,' she said bluntly. 'We've used them often in the past. Why didn't you question Samantha?'

A swift, harsh frown jagged his brow. 'She had nothing to do with the making of that necklace.'

'But she could have switched the pearls when no one was looking. I'm asking why you didn't say anything to her.'

'Are you saying,' he asked with ice in his eyes, 'that you think she was involved?'

'I find it strange that these things have started happening since she came here.'

'You could say the same of me.'

Tamara jutted her chin and stared boldly at him. 'OK, I will.'

'You actually think that I might be involved?' he rasped.

Tamara shrugged. 'It's possible.' Though she didn't really believe it. Kiel might have his faults but he wouldn't sink that low. Besides, he had no reason to. He had the best interests of the company at heart.

'I don't believe this,' he snarled, his face suffused with dark anger. 'And when I find out what has really happened I sure as hell will make you eat your words.'

He came up to her and gripped her shoulders so hard that she winced. 'I don't like being told I'm a cheat, especially by someone as imperfect as you.' His mouth turned down at the corners, his nostrils flared, and his eyes blazed into hers.

'And I don't like what you're doing to my father's company,' she retaliated sharply.

The fierce anger between them was so intense it was in danger of igniting. And added to it was a strange feeling of excitement, sexual chemistry; Tamara felt an actual desire for Kiel in this mood. Currents ran from his fingertips through the whole of her system and the next second her lips were being ground back against her teeth in a brutally punishing and bruising kiss.

'You drive me insane, Tamara. There's a little demon inside me that wants to possess you.' As he spoke there was a blazing light in his eyes and he pulled her so hard against him she thought every bone in her body was going to crack.

'Kiel,' she gasped. 'Let go of me.'

'When I'm good and ready,' he muttered harshly against her mouth, backing her against the wall so that they were not visible to the workers below. 'I don't take kindly to people casting aspersions on my character.'

'And is this how you punish them?'

'Only you, Tamara.'

With the wall behind her and Kiel in front there was no escape. All she could do was glare with icy hauteur, refusing to struggle. He would soon tire of the battle if she didn't play his game.

But she had not reckoned on Kiel's powers of persuasion. His kisses underwent a subtle change of mood. His lips moved over hers with fierce intent, not hurting now, but not gentle either. He meant business.

And when he traced the outline of her lips with his tongue, when his hands moved beneath the heavy fall of her hair to imprison the back of her head, when she felt the warmth and strength of his fingers, when his body moved with deliberate sensuality against hers, every atom of fight went out of her.

She was lost. She was lost in a world of spinning senses, of feelings and desires, of alien emotions. She was no longer a mere mortal being kissed by a man she had angered, she was soaring on another level, her body did not belong to her. This man had magical powers. She was responding against her will and yet it wasn't against her will. It was a strange, confusing, exciting, exhilarating feeling.

Her arms went around him, her mouth softened beneath the pressure of his, her heart hammered within her breast and every nerve-end was sensitised to such a degree that her whole body glowed and throbbed and wanted his touch. It had never before been so receptive to Kiel. And for it to happen here, and in such a way, was totally incredible.

He cupped her face and looked into the clear brown beauty of her eyes. With a slightly unsteady finger he traced the perfect arch of her brows and ran his finger down the length of her nose. He touched her cheek-bones and followed the shape of her ears, and finally let his fingers ride down the slender column of her throat. Though his touch was light, it burnt, it seared, and Tamara felt as though she would be branded forever.

She stood back against the wall, free to move, yet remaining there, her eyes on his face as he looked at each of her features as he touched them. 'Tamara,' he breathed hoarsely, 'let's get out of here.' He touched her breasts through the soft cashmere of her sweater and she held her breath as they swelled and hardened, and her heart pumped even faster, her throat contracting. She wanted to say yes, she wanted to go, her whole body craved for him, but she knew why he had said it. Her capitulation would be sweet revenge.

'No, Kiel.' It was the hardest decision she had ever had to make.

He pulled her fiercely to him again, one hand still on her breast, his mouth brutally claiming hers. 'Tamara, I know you feel what I feel. What's the point in fighting it?'

'Because, damn you, you know I——'

The door swung open and a startled Carol clapped a hand to her mouth. 'I'm sorry, I didn't realise, I thought you were downstairs, Kiel, I didn't know. Oh, dear.' Her face red with mortification, and looking ready to burst into tears, she fled the room.

Tamara seized the opportunity to twist out of his arms and headed for the door herself.

'Tamara, wait!'

She turned and looked at him, no trace of emotion now on her face, her chin tilted haughtily, her whole body rejecting him. It was hard doing it, very hard. Inside a fire still raged, but this was how it had to be. 'It's best, Kiel. I won't enter into the sort of relationship you want.'

'You want it too.'

'No, I don't.'

'Liar!' His eyes glittered angrily into hers. 'If we were in some other place you'd have been mine. You were ready to capitulate.' And then mockery took the place of anger. 'But I can wait, there'll be other occasions. You may go. I have this pearl problem to solve. I'll pick you up at seven-thirty for the theatre.'

Tamara looked at him sharply. 'I wasn't aware that I'd agreed to come.'

'You have no choice. Make sure you're ready.' He returned to his desk and sat down, and after staring at him furiously for a few seconds Tamara let herself out of the room.

In her own office she slumped into her chair. She had left here half an hour earlier with her sketches in her hand and a spring to her step, and now she felt as though she had been put through the rollers of an old-fashioned wringer.

She took several deep, steadying breaths and tried to restore some sort of order to her mind, but it was impossible. Round and round her thoughts went like the sails of a windmill, round and round, urged on by a mystery force. But the longer she sat there, the more muddled her mind became, and she knew it would be impossible to do any more work today.

Carol's entrance into the room was not unexpected. 'Tamara, I honestly didn't know there was anything going on between you and Kiel. I wish you'd said. Heavens, I've sat here and fantasised about him and you've never stopped me. Why didn't you say something?'

'There is nothing between me and him,' said Tamara firmly.

'But he was kissing you. I saw——'

'It meant nothing,' Tamara insisted.

'It didn't look like that to me.'

'I don't care what it looked like. I didn't want him to kiss me.'

Carol looked shocked. 'You mean he was forcing himself on you?'

'Not exactly, I suppose,' admitted Tamara, 'but the atmosphere between us after you'd gone was distinctly chilly.'

'Was it my fault?' asked Carol worriedly. 'If so, I'm sorry. I——'

Tamara checked her. 'Of course not. I was glad you interrupted.'

Carol frowned. 'I wish I understood. I've seen him with Samantha. It's all very puzzling.'

'To me as well,' said Tamara cryptically. 'Would you mind telling Kiel that I'm taking the rest of the day off?'

She did not go home; she didn't want to be alone where all she would think about was Kiel. Instead she drove into the city centre, parked her car in the multi-storey car park, and spent the whole afternoon wandering around the shops.

'Tamara!'

She whirled at the sound of her name, then groaned in disbelief when she saw Yves Delattre. He was the very last person she wanted to see.

CHAPTER SIX

'WHAT are you doing here?' Tamara asked Yves with a frown. 'Haven't you been back to Paris yet?'

'I come and go,' he said easily.

She forced a polite smile. 'I'm sorry, I haven't time to stand here talking.'

'It was such a pity that you reacted as you did. I would have liked us to be friends.' The smile that she had thought so warm and generous the first time they met now seemed false.

'I don't like people who try to force themselves on me,' she said with as much calm as she could muster. 'Please excuse me.'

But he was not ready to let her go. 'How is business these days? Is my friend, Kiel, still bringing in the orders?'

'I don't think that's anything to do with you,' she told him coldly.

'But I'm interested. Kiel is a man who always gets what he wants. At university he always got the best girls, the best results. He was good at sport, at everything he did. No matter how I tried I always came a poor second.'

And he resented that, thought Tamara. 'I'm sorry, but I'm not interested in what you have to say about Kiel. He and I are old friends, you can't surprise me. And if I hurt your feelings the other day it's your own fault for taking me back to your hotel. You knew I wanted to go home.'

'And because of your silly behaviour Kiel cancelled my order. What was he doing there anyway?' A hard note crept into his voice.

'He was concerned for my safety, if you must know,' she returned tightly. 'Apparently you have quite a reputation. Now I really must go. Goodbye, Monsieur Delattre.' And she turned and walked away with her head held high.

Kiel arrived early for their theatre date and Tamara's heart flipped at the sight of him in a dark suit she had not seen before. It sat easily on his broad shoulders, accentuating the powerful, muscular shape of him, and the grey silk shirt and spotted tie complemented it perfectly.

There was no indication on his face of the row they'd had earlier. Instead there was a smile she did not quite believe in and, as she accompanied him outside to a waiting taxi, Tamara could not quell a feeling of unease. She wished she knew what the night was going to bring.

'I thought this would be easier than trying to park in the city,' he said once they were seated, and with the glass partition firmly closed between them and the driver Tamara felt his presence fill the small space.

Always he did this, always she was totally aware of everything about him, from his clean, fresh smell to his overpowering sexuality, from his mood, which at this moment seemed to be one of amusement, to his more physical aspects, like perfectly manicured fingernails and highly polished shoes.

She crossed and uncrossed her legs, sitting well away from him in her corner, clutching her bag, unaware that her movements were giving away her inner tension.

'Relax, Tamara.' He put his hand over hers and a thousand tiny shock-waves shot through her. 'I want this to be an enjoyable evening for you.'

How was that possible, she asked herself, when she was afraid to let down her defences? It was so easy for him to get through to her, so incredibly easy. She was like putty in his hands.

She tried to pull away but he would not let her go. He sat in silence and looked at her, an enigmatic expression in the clear grey depths of his eyes, and her body grew warm as her consciousness of him increased.

He ran a finger along the length of her thigh to her knee. 'This bronzy colour suits you, and I love the feel of this material. But I don't like your hair fastened back. Why do you always do it when you know I prefer it loose? Or have you forgotten that?' There was a fractional tightening of his mouth as he reached up and began to take out the pins that held it in its neat chignon.

And to her own amazement she sat forward and let him do it, even though she knew his actions were all designed to heighten her awareness—so that by the end of the evening she would put up no resistance!

'Do you have a comb?' he asked, once her hair hung long and straight.

Tamara shook her head. Her clutch bag held only a handkerchief and some money—the few pounds were a safeguard in case she fell out with Kiel and had to find her own way home!

'In that case I'll use mine.' He combed her hair until it was as smooth as silk, seeming to find great pleasure in touching it, finally sweeping it all to one side and bringing it forward over her shoulder. It hung right down to her waist and he smoothed it over her breast.

Tamara's breathing quickened and her beautiful sloe-shaped eyes darkened with desire, despite the fact that it was a deliberate assault on her senses. Then they arrived at the Hippodrome and the moment was lost.

He bought her chocolates and in the interval they drank gin and tonic. He made no further attempt to touch her but the damage had been done. She was more conscious of him beside her than the actors on the stage. In fact she heard scarcely a word that was said.

On their way out, shoulders jostled by laughing, talking theatre-goers, she saw Yves again. He had a pretty redhead hanging on to his arm and Kiel saw him at the same time. His mouth firmed.

She said nothing until they were in a taxi being whisked to the restaurant where Kiel had booked a table. 'That's twice I've seen Yves today. I didn't know he was back in England.'

'He's rented a house. Where did you see him?' The question was sharp, his eyes narrowed and curious.

'In New Street. He stopped me.'

'Why didn't you say?'

Tamara shrugged. 'I'd forgotten, until I just saw him again. Why is he spending so much time here? Is he still hoping to place an order with you?'

'I doubt it,' said Kiel swiftly. 'But he's opening a shop here. What did he want you for?'

'To pass the time of day, I presume.'

'Yves doesn't pass the time of day with anyone, especially beautiful girls,' he said tersely. 'Come on, Tamara, you can do better than that.'

She lifted her shoulders. 'He asked what you were doing in his hotel and how your business was doing, that's all. Nothing very much.'

'What did you tell him?'

'That you were protecting me—because of his reputation.'

Kiel swore. 'He wouldn't like that. What was his reaction?'

'I didn't wait for one, I walked away.'

The taxi stopped at that moment and they entered the restaurant, and to her relief Yves wasn't mentioned again.

'What did Briggs say about the pearls?' she asked as they were waiting for their main course. She hadn't meant to talk business but there was a lull in the conversation and she could think of nothing else to say.

'They're as sure as they can possibly be that the pearls they supplied us with were genuine. They have some more in stock from the same source and they've checked them.'

'So what are you going to do now?'

His eyes looked troubled. 'I don't know. I suppose I ought to bring in the police but I'm a bit reluctant at this stage.'

'But someone's doing it.' She thought he was insane not involving them, unless he was covering up? She still could not get Samantha out of her mind. It was too much of a coincidence that these things had started happening since she had joined the firm.

And it was also too much of a coincidence that Samantha Sheldon was at that moment walking across the room towards them. Tamara's eyes widened as she saw the girl.

'Kiel, I didn't know you were eating here.' She deliberately ignored Tamara.

He frowned. 'Are you alone, Sam?' The idea seemed to displease him.

'I was with a friend,' she admitted, 'but she just left. I was going too when I saw you and Tamara. May I join you?'

He glanced at Tamara and she wondered what thoughts were going through his mind. He had hoped tonight might be the night he would make love to her and now Samantha was in danger of ruining his plans.

'I don't mind.' She smiled easily, lying through her teeth because she minded very much. Samantha Sheldon was the last person she wanted at their table.

He nodded at the other girl. 'Of course.' And he caught the head waiter's eye.

Another chair was brought to the table. 'Can I get you a drink, Sam?'

Her smile was brilliant. 'I'd love a brandy, if you're sure it's no trouble?'

Samantha played up to Kiel for all she was worth, ignoring Tamara, talking only to him, sometimes putting her hand on his arm as she spoke. And she saw to it that the conversation was about people and places that Tamara knew nothing about.

Once or twice her eyes met Tamara's and there was triumph in them, also a veiled warning. Tamara sat back and listened, trying to stifle her jealousy, wondering whether she ought to silently thank Samantha for rescuing her. Fighting off Kiel's advances would not have been easy in the aroused mood she had been in. Of course that had all gone now. She was filled with passion of a different kind.

'Is something wrong?' Kiel looked at her and saw the glitter in her eyes.

'I'm ready to go home,' she said bluntly.

'Can I beg a lift?' asked Samantha at once.

'I'm not in my car, I have to order a taxi,' he said. 'I'll order you one too.'

'But surely we could all go together? Doesn't Tamara live en route to my place?'

He hesitated only a fraction of a second. 'Sure; excuse me a moment.'

For the first time Samantha gave Tamara her full attention. 'What are you doing out with Kiel?'

Tamara's fine brows lifted at the acidity of her tone. 'Isn't it obvious—we were having a cosy evening.'

'But he told me that you're only like brother and sister.'

'He did?' Tamara hid a smile. 'He must have been pulling your leg. That was a long time ago. Things have changed between us since then.'

'Then I'll have to see that they change back again, and it won't be difficult,' said Samantha spitefully. 'I can take him off you any time I like.'

Tamara did not doubt that. What Kiel felt for her was nothing more than lust. He definitely had more of an affinity with Samantha. She saw that for herself every single day.

'If you're ready, ladies, our taxi is waiting.' Kiel smiled down at them, but Tamara noticed that it was on Samantha his eyes rested longest. He had already tired of his game with her. That would wait for another day.

They all three sat on the back seat, Kiel between them, and this time there was no corner to shrink into. Tamara remained silent, her ankles neatly crossed, her chin high, her bag clutched on her lap, staring straight ahead. Samantha, on the other hand, talked incessantly, turning to Kiel, touching him, her eyes on him all the time. It was a blatant picture of a girl out to get her man.

Nor did Kiel seem to mind. He gave her his full attention, smiling often, his tone gentle when he spoke. There were none of the harsh tones that he adopted when speaking to Tamara. It just showed how much he really hated her, she thought, when he could switch his attention to this other girl at the flutter of an eyelash.

When they reached Tamara's house Kiel insisted on accompanying her to the door and making sure she was safely inside.

'Thank you,' she said, 'but there was no need.'

'You know I don't like you being alone here.'

Tamara frowned. 'I thought I'd convinced you that I was coping and there are no problems.'

'Let's say it's my chivalrous streak.'

'Well, thank you for your old-fashioned courtesy,' she said sharply, 'but both your carriage and your lady-friend are waiting. Goodnight, Kiel.'

'Tonight hasn't turned out exactly how I planned,' he growled.

'What a pity,' she answered brightly. 'But I'm sure Samantha will make an excellent substitute. And she'll be far more willing.'

His eyes narrowed. 'Sarcasm doesn't suit you. You'd have been willing all right, and don't try to deny it. But there'll be other times, Tamara, don't worry about that. I might even come back tonight after I've seen Samantha safely home.'

'You'll find the doors locked and bolted,' she warned him, her eyes flashing. 'Your key won't be much good then. And as far as I'm concerned Samantha's done me a good turn. I hate ugly scenes, and that's what would have happened if you'd tried to make love to me.'

His lips curved in a knowing smile. 'Really, Tamara, don't try to delude yourself. You know as well as I do that your body was ready for mine.'

Without actually lying Tamara could not deny it. She tilted her chin and eyed him coldly. 'Not as ready as I'm sure Samantha's is.'

'There's no fun in bedding a girl who offers it to you on a plate,' he sneered.

'But there is fun in chasing someone who's unwilling. Is that what you're saying?'

'Not at all. You're only playing at being unwilling.'

'Like you're playing at wanting me when all the time you hate my guts.'

Kiel stiffened at this reminder, but at the same time the taxi driver hooted his horn and he swung away without another word.

As she got ready for bed Tamara could not help thinking about Kiel and Samantha and what they were doing. Samantha would not have let him get away with seeing her to the door. He was probably inside now and they were—— She cut short her thoughts in anger. She wouldn't think about them; she *wouldn't*.

Early the next morning her mother telephoned. 'Is something wrong?' asked Tamara at once.

'No, love, of course not. I wanted to catch you before you went to work. I tried to ring last night but there was no answer.'

'I went out with Kiel.'

'Oh, Tamara, that's good, I am pleased. It was your father's dream that one day you and Kiel would grow to love one another.'

'There's no chance of that,' she told her mother bitterly. 'None at all.'

'But it's a beginning, surely? He wanted nothing to do with you after the accident.'

How could she tell her mother that he was simply after retribution? 'We're still not very close, Mummy. Please don't think we are. When are you coming back?'

'I'm not sure. I'm actually thinking about moving in with Ida permanently.'

'Oh!'

'You are all right on your own, aren't you?' asked her mother anxiously.

'Of course I am, it was just a surprise, that's all.' More than a surprise—an absolute shock.

'I'll let you know when I've made up my mind. Look after yourself, Tammy, I'll ring again soon.'

Tamara had never envisaged her mother moving away completely. She had thought it was a temporary thing until she had got over Ben's death. From having both her parents around her for so long she was now going to be left all on her own.

When she went to the office she watched Samantha closely. The girl seemed to have an extra glow about her, confirming, in Tamara's mind, that something had happened last night, and every nerve-end tightened in anger and jealousy.

It was ridiculous feeling like this when she didn't want him herself. It should have made it easier to fight her attraction, but somehow it made it harder. Especially when she saw how gentle Kiel was with Samantha. She wondered whether he was taking her out at night.

Her own evenings were spent in solitude. Occasionally she called on Patti and Rory, but often she spent her time cleaning and polishing, and laundering her clothes. Her mother had always done the housework herself, never wanting or needing a daily cleaner. Tamara found it very hard after a full day at the office.

The garden, too, had awoken after its winter's sleep and needed attention, and early one evening when she was struggling to start the lawnmower she heard a sound behind her.

'You look as though you could do with some help.' Kiel, in khaki cotton trousers and a thin sweater, stood looking at her.

Her stomach fluttered helplessly at the sight of him, her skin warming and prickling as it always did whenever he was near. But she hid her torment and glared at him, giving the starting cord another furious pull. To her dismay it came off in her hand!

'Here, let me.' He stepped closer and took the cord, his fingers brushing hers, sensitising her skin, causing her pulse to quicken erratically. Then he stooped down to rethread and secure it and she was able to back away. 'Don't you think you should employ a gardener?' he asked. 'There's far too much for you to do alone.'

'I might not be living here much longer,' she told him. Why did he always do this? Why did he always project this aura of power over her?

'You're moving?' asked Kiel sharply, looking up abruptly. 'Where? Why? Isn't this rather sudden?'

As their eyes met her stomach tightened and she wondered if it would be like this for the rest of her life. She knew he was thinking she might be quitting her job as well and that he would lose the pleasure of seeking his revenge, and she was tempted to let him go on thinking it. But she shrugged and said simply, 'I might have to. My mother's thinking of moving in with her sister permanently, in which case this house will be far too big.'

'I see.' His frown faded. 'Have you a screwdriver?'

It was a relief to get away from him for a few seconds. She drew several deep, steadying breaths, reminding herself that Samantha was the love of his life, she was merely a plaything, and found what he needed in her father's toolbox in the garage.

She stood and watched as he fixed the mower. His hair was a little longer these days and she liked it better. When it was brutally short it made him look tougher and rougher, like a commando. Not that the edges of him were softened at all—he still had the power to hurt with a look or a word.

Finally he straightened his back, gave the cord one pull, and the motor started. Tamara grimaced. Why did men always make it look so easy?

'I'll do the lawns,' he said. 'You can make me a cup of coffee.'

She was given no choice, and from the kitchen window she watched him walking up and down. There was a domesticity about the scene that she found oddly appealing. If only things had been different between them, she thought. If she hadn't resented him almost all her life, if her father hadn't left him the business and caused an even bigger rift, if Anna hadn't died the way she had. *If, if if . . .*

Why was she so attracted to him? Why couldn't she get him out of her mind? Why did he affect her to the point when she almost felt like screaming? And what was the point in thinking about him in those terms when his resentment of her would never go away? She turned back to the kettle which had long ago cut out, pressing the button and waiting for it to reboil.

The coffee made, she took it out into the garden, and he joined her at the table on the terrace. It was a cool evening and it would soon be dark, but she felt none of the chill in the air. All she felt was this man's presence. Even the very air around him seemed to crackle.

'Tell me more about your mother moving in with her sister. When did she tell you that?'

Tamara pulled herself together. 'The other morning over the phone.'

'I know she took your father's death badly, but I never thought she'd move from this house.'

'It's full of happy memories, I know that,' said Tamara, 'but I can understand how she feels. She's never lived here without Daddy.'

'They always made me so welcome. This was my second home. I'll be sad to see it sold. Where will you go, Tamara?'

She lifted her shoulders. 'I don't know. I haven't given it any thought yet. I don't think Mummy's actually made up her mind.'

'Anna liked it here too.' The words came out slowly and quietly as his thoughts winged back over the years.

Tamara closed her eyes momentarily, feeling the automatic tightening of her muscles whenever he brought up his sister's name. It seemed that wherever they went, whatever they did, some memory was always triggered off.

'She used to beg me to bring her here so that she could play with you in the garden or swim in the pool.' His eyes moved across to the blue pool, still covered until the weather got warmer, and they narrowed as fresh thoughts invaded, until with a snort of anger he pushed himself up. 'I'd better finish before it gets dark.'

He didn't even look at her as he left the table, but Tamara felt the impact of his hostility as much as if he had slayed her with words. She put the mugs back on the tray and went indoors. She hadn't asked him to do the lawns, he didn't have to come here, he didn't have to arouse memories. It was all his own fault. Why take it out on her?

By the time he had finished, cleaned the mower and put it away, it was dark. Tamara's supper was almost cooked and she felt obliged to ask him to stay.

'It's only lamb chops, I'm afraid, but you're welcome to share what I have.' She hoped he would say no; indeed, she felt sure he would. He still looked in a far from civilised mood.

'Thank you, I will. I'll just wash my hands.'

He disappeared from the kitchen and Tamara tried to steady her pulsing nerves. Always he surprised her. When he came back everything was ready. The kitchen table laid for two, the plates heated, the potatoes and vegetables drained.

'I hope you don't mind eating in here? It's a habit I've got into since Mummy left.' Even to her own ears her voice sounded stilted.

'It's fine by me,' he said agreeably, 'but Ben wouldn't have been happy. He always liked to do things properly.'

'That's when we were a family.'

'It's hard to lose the ones you love.'

Tamara had her back to him but she heard the now familiar condemnation in his voice. 'But life has to go on, Kiel. Changes have to be accepted.'

'Your father had a heart attack, I can accept that, but Anna's death was needless and unpardonable.'

With an unsteady hand Tamara slapped his plate down in front of him. 'I didn't have to invite you to stay, Kiel, and I don't have to take this from you.'

His eyes locked bitterly into hers. 'Can I help it if every time I look at you I think of what you did to my sister?'

And is that what you're thinking when you want to make love to me? she wanted to ask, but she didn't. 'I don't suppose you can help thinking it,' she whipped instead, 'but you don't have to keep throwing it at me. I had nightmares for weeks and weeks after the accident and they're beginning to come back, thanks to you. Why have you come here tonight?'

'Ah, yes, I'd almost forgotten. I'm thinking of throwing a party—I wondered if you'd like to come?'

Tamara looked at him suspiciously. 'Why invite me when there's no love lost between us?'

'Let's say I thought it might be—interesting.'

Tamara felt sure he was hatching some heinous plot. 'Will Samantha be there?'

'Naturally.'

'Then thank you, but no.'

His eyes hardened. 'I want you there, Tamara. I've invited Patti and her boyfriend as well.'

'You've already asked her?' questioned Tamara disbelievingly. 'But you hardly know her.' He had done this deliberately so that she wouldn't be able to refuse.

'I don't think that matters, and it certainly didn't matter to Patti—she jumped at the chance.'

'I suppose I'll come, then,' said Tamara ungraciously. 'When is it to be?'

'On Saturday.'

It wasn't until he was ready to leave, after a meal that he had eaten in an uncomfortable silence so far as Tamara had been concerned, though Kiel had seemed to have some secret thoughts that had kept him amused, that he said to her, 'Oh, by the way, it's fancy dress. A masked ball on a moderate scale.'

Her eyes flashed. 'You haven't given me much time to work out what to wear.'

'I'm sure you'll think of something original,' he taunted. 'I'll see you on Saturday, then, at about eight?'

She frowned. 'Not before then?'

'No, I'll be out of the country.'

No explanation, so she had no idea whether it was business or pleasure that was taking him abroad.

At the front door he turned and looked at her, and for a moment the hardness had gone out of his eyes. 'You might find this difficult to believe, but I'm going to miss you.'

'You mean you're going to miss tormenting me?' she flashed.

'You're a very beautiful girl. You're good to have around.' The words seemed to be coming out against his will. Tamara's breath caught in her throat, but she knew it was unwise to read anything into the words. He desired her, yes, it was there in his eyes, but there were no emotions involved. It was nothing but a strong, physical need.

Yet despite this knowledge she felt herself leaning towards him, and when his mouth came down on hers it was as though he had put a match to her and set her on fire. The kiss was disappointingly brief, though, and the light in Kiel's eyes told her that he knew exactly what feelings were ripping through her. 'Till Saturday,' he said softly. The door opened and closed and he was gone.

Tamara stood a moment, her fingers to her mouth, still feeling the heat of his body and her own traitorous response. 'Damn you, Kiel Kramer,' she cried out aloud. 'What right have you to do this to me?'

She marched back into the kitchen and began to clear the table with quick, angry movements, then suddenly she left everything and crossed to the telephone on the kitchen wall. She dialled and waited.

'Patti?' she demanded, the second it was picked up.

'It's Rory, she's in the shower. Is that you, Tamara? Is it important?'

'It's about this damned party of Kiel's. I——'

'Oh, yes, what a sport to ask us. It sounds a great idea. Patti was going to ring you. She wants to know what you're going to wear.'

Tamara slumped against the wall. He sounded so excited there was no point in asking them to forget it. 'I don't know yet, I've only just found out.'

'Maybe we could go as the Three Musketeers?'

'No, I don't think so.' A faint smile curved her lips. 'It doesn't sound like me. I'll get in touch with Patti some other time. Bye, Rory.'

Apparently everyone at Wilding Jewellery had been invited to Kiel's party. It was the whole topic of conversation for the rest of the week.

Tamara missed him. Tricky though their relationship was, it added something to her life. It was as if a flame had gone out and she found herself actually looking forward to Saturday.

Word seemed to have spread about the emeralds and the pearls. Several orders were cancelled and Tamara worried about what it was going to do to their business. She still found it difficult to think of it as Kiel's and not her father's, and she took as much interest as if it were her own.

On Friday afternoon Samantha sauntered into her office. 'I can't wait until tomorrow night. It's really going to be some party. Who are you going as?'

'If I told you, wouldn't that be defeating the whole idea of a masked ball?' asked Tamara coldly. 'Half the fun is guessing who is who.'

'I'm actually surprised Kiel asked you.'

Tamara frowned. 'Why shouldn't he? He's invited everyone else who works for him.'

'But there is a difference, isn't there?' she insisted.

Tamara's eyes narrowed. 'In what way?'

'Let's say I've found out a little more about you. All that talk about something going on between you and Kiel was a pack of lies, wasn't it? How could any man love a girl who had killed his sister?'

Tamara gasped and felt herself go cold. 'I don't know who told you that, and I don't want to know, but I do know that you're not welcome in my office.'

'If I were Kiel I wouldn't even want you working here. You must be a perpetual reminder of——'

'Get out!' Tamara's eyes blazed with anger and loathing. *'Get out!'*

Samantha smiled and walked slowly back to the door. 'OK, I'm going. Did Kiel tell you that he's asked me to be his hostess tomorrow night? It speaks for itself which one of us he prefers, don't you think?'

The door closed with maddening softness behind her and Tamara picked up the first object that came to hand, which happened to be a stapler, and hurled it at the door. It left a small indentation, a permanent reminder of her fury, and then slid to the floor.

Samantha's statement had been timed to perfection. Tamara wouldn't see the girl again now until the party, and then she would have to suffer the humiliation of seeing her at Kiel's side, greeting guests and carrying out all the other duties of a hostess. Tamara wished there were some way she could get out of it, but Patti was in raptures over the whole idea and she did not want to let her friend down.

She had given a lot of thought as to what she would wear. Her friends were going as Harlequin and Columbine, though Tamara doubted Rory would be able to mime his way through the whole evening, and they had suggested she go as Snow White, because of her black hair. But that would make her too obvious. She did not want to be immediately recognised, especially by Kiel. And in the end she decided to dress up as Marilyn Monroe. With a blonde wig and bright make-up she would be totally unlike her normal self.

A taxi took the three of them to Henley-in-Arden. Cars were already filling the drive and couples drifting in. Mask in place, Tamara followed, effecting a Marilyn Monroe wiggle in her tight, low-cut dress and very high heels. The door stood wide open and there was no Kiel or Samantha to welcome them, so at least the first obstacle was overcome.

Two rooms had been opened into one by folding back partitioning doors, and there were already at least two dozen people present. Tamara's eyes searched for Kiel. Was that him in the Robin Hood outfit? And was the Maid Marion hanging on to his arm Samantha? Or was that him over there, the Barber of Seville, twirling his cut-throat razor? Or even King Charles in his elaborate wig? To her consternation, she couldn't tell. Perhaps he wasn't in the room at all?

She wandered about, smiling, nodding, not knowing who any of them were. The masks were an effective disguise. Until she felt a hand on the back of her neck, and a prickle of pleasure ran right down her spine. She would know Kiel's touch any time, anywhere.

'Don't look,' he whispered warningly in her ear when she attempted to turn around.

'But how did you know it was me?' she asked. She had thought her disguise complete. She was so unlike her usual self, even Patti had said she couldn't recognise her.

'Because you're a wickedly irresistible lady, Tamara. I'd know you anywhere in any guise, and you're wearing the perfume that always arouses my animal instincts. Didn't you know that? I think tonight might be the night.'

There was no mistaking his meaning and Tamara gasped, whirling around, ready with a quick snub, but she was alone. He had melted into the sea of masked faces.

CHAPTER SEVEN

TAMARA enjoyed the party more than she had thought possible. The furniture had been cleared and music played. She was invited to dance by Charlie Chaplin, Tarzan, and then Hitler, who she discovered to her delight was Bill Pearce. 'I thought it was you,' she said, 'though I couldn't be sure.'

'I can't recognise anyone,' she laughed, 'not even Kiel. Do you know which one he is?'

'I do,' he smiled, 'but I don't think we're allowed to say until the unmasking at midnight. But it's certainly some party. I've never seen so much food and drink.' A table was groaning beneath the weight of a finger buffet to be eaten later, and beer and spirits were flowing freely.

Paul turned out to be another Harlequin—there were three of them altogether, two of them absolutely identical—and she could see Rory entertaining a growing group of people with an elaborate mime. She hadn't realised he was so eloquent with his hands and body movements.

She still thought Samantha might be Maid Marion and she kept her eye on Robin Hood. He was certainly the right build, and both of them were circulating freely, as though it was their duty to make sure everyone was happy and lacked for nothing.

Patti sought her out a little while later. 'I'm having a wonderful time,' she said. 'Kiel sure knows how to throw a party. Which one is he? I want to thank him for inviting us.'

Tamara shrugged. 'You'll have to wait, I don't know either.'

'You don't?' Patti sounded disbelieving. 'I thought the vibes would draw the two of you together.'

'He found me,' admitted Tamara, 'but he stood behind and wouldn't let me look.'

'Which means,' said Patti dramatically, 'that it's right what I've thought all along. He is interested in you. If he wasn't aware of everything there is to know about you he wouldn't have recognised you.'

Tamara shrugged and laughed it off, but if that were true, though she doubted it very much, why couldn't she recognise Kiel when her attraction for him was so much stronger?

And then it was time to eat and everyone surged forward. Tamara was wedged in the crowd unable to move when Kiel's voice in her ear sent a further prickle of sensation through every nerve-end.

'Are you enjoying the party?'

His hands held the sides of her head so that she could not look around, but she could feel the whole, hard length of him pressed up against her and everyone else faded into oblivion.

'Yes, I am,' she said. 'We all are. They're saying what a marvellous time they are having. What made you decide on it?'

'I think everyone needs to let their hair down occasionally. We're all guilty of working too hard and not having enough fun. Anna would have loved this, she enjoyed dressing up.' His body went tense as he spoke, his hands tightening until her head felt as though it were clamped in a vice. 'Her life was only just beginning. She's missed out on so much.'

'Dammit, Kiel,' snapped Tamara savagely, 'do you think I don't know all these things?'

'I'm going to make sure you never forget. I have to live in this house, Tamara. I see her every day, I hear her laughter, I go to bed at night and I think about her. When my parents died I made it my duty to look after her, and I failed, and all because of you.'

Tamara clenched her teeth and remained silent. Why didn't he ever let up? Why was he insisting on making her life hell?

'Have you nothing further to say?'

'What's the point?' she whispered furiously. 'All I can say is that if my father had known that you were going to treat me like this he'd never have left you the business.'

'Ben would have liked us to fall in love and get married,' he snorted.

'Don't I know it?' she snapped. 'But that's as likely as the moon falling out of the sky.'

'It could be a solution.'

'What do you mean?' She asked the question sharply, yet even so the thought of being married to Kiel turned her into a quivering mass. To live with him, to sleep with him, to be made love to by him. To have him love her unequivocably. It was a dream, a far-fetched dream that would never, ever see the light of day.

'Then you would be completely at my mercy.'

A shiver ran through her. 'And you'd like that, wouldn't you? You'd like to spend the rest of your life destroying me.'

His hands slackened and she was free and she stood and waited for his reaction, but when none came she turned around and only Rory stood behind her. She hoped he hadn't overheard their conversation.

After the buffet she danced with Paul, and Bill again, and several other men she did not know, and she tried to push Kiel out of her mind. But it was impossible. And when midnight drew near she found herself waiting breathlessly.

She was watching Robin Hood and could not believe her eyes when she discovered it wasn't Kiel after all. Her eyes roved the crowd and finally she saw him. *Harlequin!* In exactly the same costume as Rory. So had it been he standing behind her at the buffet table? Tamara frowned and at that moment Samantha spoke at her side.

'Surprised? I've seen you looking for Kiel all night.'

And Samantha, as Columbine, had been with him most of the time. Tamara had seen them and dismissed them and now she was not sure whether it was Rory or Kiel who had been entertaining the guests. She did not like to think that she had not been able to tell him and her tone was sharp as she answered. 'You must have been mistaken. I knew exactly who Kiel was. Didn't you see him talking to me?'

It was clear by Samantha's frown that she had been unaware of the attention he had paid Tamara.

'Oh, yes,' Tamara went on cruelly, 'Kiel made sure I wasn't feeling neglected.'

Samantha's eyes flashed dangerously. 'You're lying!'

'Why should I do that?'

'Because you're jealous of the fact that he chose me to help him organise this party.'

Tamara shook her head. 'I'm never jealous of anything Kiel does. We don't have that kind of a relationship.'

'As far as I can see you don't have any kind of a relationship. He despises you.'

'Has he told you that himself?' asked Tamara coldly.

Samantha shrugged. 'Not exactly, but it's easy to see what you've done to him.'

'Excuse me,' Tamara's eyes were icy cold, 'my friend is calling.' She left Samantha and crossed over to Patti. 'That woman's a bitch,' she said bitterly.

'Who? What woman?' Patti frowned.

'Samantha Sheldon. Somehow she's found out about Anna and she doesn't lose any opportunity to remind me of what I did.'

Patti's eyes shone a furious green. 'How dare she? Who told her? Kiel?'

Tamara shrugged.

'I think it's time we left. I'll ask Rory to phone for a taxi.'

But while they were waiting Kiel came up to Tamara and invited her to dance. It was the first time that evening and she couldn't believe it. She wasn't sure that she wanted to, but she walked into his arms anyway.

He held her close and her whole body screamed out to be made love to. Friends or enemies, whatever they were, it made no difference to the way she reacted. She felt right in his arms, and she could not help wondering whether Kiel would have felt the same way about her if it hadn't been for the accident.

And then Rory indicated that they should go and she freed herself. 'I'm sorry, but Rory's ordered a taxi. I'm leaving now. Thank you for inviting me. It was a wonderful party.'

Kiel took her arm firmly. 'You're going nowhere yet. If necessary I'll run you home myself, but I'd prefer you to stay the night.' He ignored her gasp and led her across to her friends. 'Tamara's staying,' he said abruptly.

Patti's eyes widened and she looked at Tamara with a questioning frown and then shrugged. 'It's your prerogative. Have fun. Thanks for a marvellous evening, Kiel.' And she and Rory left.

Kiel took Tamara into his arms again and they moved to the taped music, and as one tune finished and another began he showed no signs of letting her go.

By this time Tamara's whole body pulsed with need and pleasure and when she caught Samantha's eye and saw her angry scowl she merely smiled and turned her face up to Kiel.

There was an instant's surprise in his eyes at her obvious invitation, but the next second his mouth came down on hers. The kiss was brief but utterly sensual, and it aroused feelings Tamara knew she ought to quell but could not.

She moved her body against his and felt the hardness of him and the thud of his heart and wished again that things were different between them.

'Let's get out of this crush,' he muttered harshly, but it was not until they were in the hall and heading upstairs that she realised exactly what he meant.

'Kiel, *no!*' Her tone was urgent.

His face darkened. 'Don't try that game with me, Tamara. You've been tempting me all evening in that dress.' His eyes flickered over the swell of her breasts in the tight-fitting bodice, then lifted to her face. 'And you've been wondering which of those costumed figures was me, whether I was near you, watching you, wanting you.'

'No. . .' There was faint panic in her voice.

'Don't deny it, I know it's true. And you were right, I have been watching you—and I want you.'

'But you can't leave your guests, it wouldn't be right.'

'Can't I?'

'Some of them will be going shortly, you ought to be here to receive their thanks and say goodbye.'

'You're right,' he grinned, 'let's prolong the pleasure, or the agony, whichever way you like to look at it. Come, we will dance again.'

And when he left her to say goodbye to his guests she would slip away, thought Tamara.

But it didn't work out like that; he kept her beside him for the rest of the evening, even when he was seeing his guests off. Samantha was furious, but it made Tamara wonder whether she had been lying when she'd said Kiel had asked her to act as hostess.

He even ordered a taxi for Samantha so that she had no choice except to leave when the last of them went, and finally they were alone. Completely alone. And Tamara felt apprehension rip through her.

Kiel had planned this all along, she felt sure, and she wished now that she had never agreed to come. Not that she didn't feel a bodily need for him—she did, urgently—but not like this, not when his reasons for wanting to make love to her were the wrong ones.

He took her through into the kitchen and sat her down on a chair while he made coffee. Tamara had not realised how tired she was until then. She put her head back and closed her eyes, listening to the chink of china and the rattle of spoons, feeling Kiel's presence.

When all was suddenly silent she looked up and found him watching her. Their eyes met and held and her stomach contracted, and it was hard hiding her feelings from him.

'Are you tired?' There was unexpected concern in his voice.

Tamara frowned. 'Would you care if I was? Would it make any difference? Or are you still intent on having your evil way with me?'

His eyes narrowed. 'Is that how you see it?'

'What other interpretation can I put on your threat?'

'A mutual need perhaps?'

Tamara's chin lifted. 'I don't need you, Kiel.'

'No? I think you do.'

It was said with such conviction that Tamara shot up out of her chair. 'No, I don't. Not now, not ever. Please take me home.'

'When I'm ready. Relax, Tamara.' He walked over to her and put his hands on her shoulders, looking deep into her eyes.

'This is insanity,' she protested.

'Insanity denying what we both want and feel and need?'

'You never give up, do you?' she muttered. 'Let go of me, Kiel, I want to order a taxi.'

'If you still feel the same way in ten minutes' time, you can go,' he said.

Tamara frowned.

'I mean it.'

She didn't trust him, and when his fingers began caressing her softly perfumed skin she knew she was right. He was giving himself ten minutes to seduce her—and if he carried on touching her like this it would take only two!

But she did not stop him when his mouth nuzzled her ear, when his warm, moist tongue tantalised. Her body had a will of its own where Kiel was concerned.

He was the only man who had ever been able to arouse her so completely.

His eyes were glazed with desire as their lips met, and during the long, mind-shattering kiss she felt once again the hardness of his thighs, the pounding beat of his heart, the depth of his arousal, and her mouth opened to accept his deepening kiss. Her arms went around him, her hands splaying over the silk of his Harlequin suit, feeling his hard, muscular strength.

His kisses became more urgent; and soft, animal whimpers escaped the back of Tamara's throat. When he undid the zip at the back of her dress and pulled it down over her shoulders she raised no objection. The percolator was bubbling and gurgling but neither heard; they were conscious only of a deep, urgent, pagan need for each other.

He lowered his head to kiss her breasts and Tamara's fingers curled tightly into his hair. Her body jerked spasmodically as her arousal deepened and it seemed forever that he kissed her, teasing her nipples with his teeth and tongue, returning to take her mouth, and then back again to her breasts. He was driving her insane.

The percolator sighed and was silent, and at the same time Kiel seemed to come to his senses, thrusting her roughly and unexpectedly and disappointingly from him. 'You're right, Tamara,' he growled fiercely. 'This is insanity. How can I make love to you when you're my sister's killer?'

Tamara flinched as though he had struck her, and she glared at him as she pulled her dress back into position. Then she lifted her chin and managed to say haughtily, 'I'm glad you've come to your senses. Now may I ring for that taxi?'

'I'll take you.'

He strode across the kitchen and Tamara suddenly saw the incongruity of the situation. Kiel, in his boldly coloured Harlequin outfit, looked less like a lover than she had ever seen him. She began to laugh and once started could not stop.

He turned and looked at her with cold disapproval. 'Would you like to share the joke?'

She shook her head. 'I'm sorry, it's—it's just the way you're dressed.'

'If it affords you that much amusement I'll get changed.' He took the stairs two at a time and when he came back his face was a blank mask, his tone hard. 'Are you ready?'

She was not sure whether he was angry with himself or with her and she was no longer amused. She nodded and followed him out to his car. As on so many occasions there was an uncomfortable silence between them, and when he pulled up outside her house he said harshly, 'Remind me how much I hate you if I'm ever in danger of getting carried away again.'

Tamara said nothing. What was there to say?

After making sure she was safely inside he roared away down the road, and by this time Tamara was angry too. She had asked for none of this. He had invited her to the party, he had made all the suggestions, done all the running, and now he was blaming it on her.

Her blood was boiling as she hurried upstairs to her bedroom, and her hands shaking as she stripped off the dress. It was evident that things weren't going to get any better between them—in fact there was every sign that they would get worse. She was more sorely tempted than ever to hand in her notice. How could she carry on working for a swine like Kiel? Only the thought that she would be letting down her father stopped her.

She pulled on her nightie, snapped off the light and climbed into bed, settling herself comfortably, determined to push all thoughts of Kiel Kramer out of her mind. But it was a sheer impossibility. He invaded her thoughts, as he had done for most of her life. He was the most attractive man she had ever met and yet fate had decreed that there would always be an insurmountable barrier between them.

Sleep would not come. She punched the pillows, got out of bed and opened the window, but still she tossed and turned, her body restless, yearning for a man she could not have.

When sleep did finally claim her she was tormented by shadowy, meaningless dreams and she awoke feeling tired and out of sorts. Thank goodness it was Sunday.

She spent the whole day weeding the garden, needing to vent her anger on hard, physical work. But it was a task that did not need a lot of concentration and Kiel was constantly in her thoughts.

How much pleasure did he get, she wondered, out of hurting her with his constant references to Anna and the way she had died? Was it affording him the satisfaction he craved? Or were these perpetual reminders adding to his torment? If only he would let go, if only he would accept that it had been an unfortunate accident and leave it at that.

In the days that followed Kiel spoke to Tamara only when strictly necessary, and this hurt her more than he would ever know. Seeing him, being with him, knowing nothing would ever come of it, was nothing less than torture.

She was also disturbed because more and more orders were being cancelled, suggesting that somehow their customers had found out about the pearls and emeralds. Her father would have been worried sick if he were still alive. Nothing like this had ever happened to him.

The meeting with Princess Margherita loomed nearer and Tamara began to feel nervous about that as well. What if she didn't like her designs? What if she said some absolutely awful things about them?

And what should Tamara wear? She had never mixed with royalty before. Should she buy something new? Then common sense asserted itself. This was a business meeting, for goodness' sake. She had plenty of smart suits. Why was she being so sensitive?

Then on Monday Kiel called her into his office. He sat at his desk, sleeves rolled up, his fingers toying with a pencil. 'Are you ill, Tamara?'

She frowned. 'Of course not. What makes you say that?'

'You've lost weight!' It was more an accusation than a statement.

Was it any wonder when she lay awake every night thinking about him? When she only pecked at her food and wished time and time again that her father had not put her into this difficult situation? The trouble was, the more she tried to push him out of her mind, the more she thought about him. 'I'm surprised you noticed.' He never seemed to look at her these days.

'I'm aware of every breath you draw, Tamara.'

It was a sweeping statement, and for the first time since his party she allowed herself to look directly into the cool greyness of his eyes. It was fatal. Her stomach

churned, pulses skidded, her heart went into top gear.
And in that moment Tamara knew she was in danger
of falling in love. Perhaps she already was? Perhaps
it was more than physical attraction that she felt? She
looked away quickly, but not before he had seen her
vulnerability.

'Aren't you eating properly, Tamara? Aren't you
bothering to cook yourself proper meals now that your
mother's no longer there to do it for you?'

'Why should it interest you?' she asked him bluntly.
'Or is it that you're afraid my work might suffer?'

'That could be a problem,' he admitted. 'We're in
enough trouble as it is at the moment. But, hard as
you might find it to accept, I was actually thinking
about you.'

'Why?' she demanded. 'When has my health ever
been any concern of yours?'

'You're Ben's daughter.' He said it as though it
answered everything.

'You mean your conscience is bothering you?' she
suggested critically.

His brows drew together in a fierce frown. 'Why
should it?'

'Why shouldn't it?' she demanded. 'The way you've
been treating me I'm surprised it's not you who hasn't
been sleeping at night. You might admit it's not what
my father would have wanted.'

His nostrils flared as he looked at her through half-
closed eyes. 'Ben didn't realise how hard Anna's death
hit me.'

'You mean you very carefully kept your feelings
hidden. But now he's no longer here you feel no such
need. You're quite happy to slam into me at every
opportunity.'

His mouth was grim and thin, a muscle jerked in his jaw. 'Dammit, Tamara, can I help how I feel?'

'You could control it,' she told him bitterly. 'You're making my life hell, do you know that?'

He smiled thinly and she could almost hear him congratulating himself. 'Then that makes two of us. I've been living my own private hell ever since Anna died.'

She took a deep, angry breath. 'Is that why you've called me in here, to tell me that? To have another go at me?'

He glanced at her impatiently. 'I don't even know how we got on to the subject. I'm worried that you're not eating properly. I'll pick you up tonight and buy you dinner.'

'No, thanks.' Her chin lifted, her back stiffened. 'I've made other plans.'

'Then change them,' he snarled.

'I have no wish to. You can take out Samantha instead. What's happened to the two of you? I haven't seen her in here so often lately.' Since the party, in fact. 'Have you fallen out?'

'Samantha never meant anything to me.'

He could have fooled her. 'Nor have I, so far as I know. So why the insistence?'

'You need someone to look after you.'

She eyed him coldly. 'And you're nominating yourself? I'd rather die from lack of nutrition than put up with your company. You're forgetting I've had a taste of your treatment—and I don't like it. Thanks for the concern, Kiel, but it's not welcome.' With that she walked out of his office.

It surprised her that he did not call her back, that he let her go without another word, but at seven that evening he appeared on her doorstep.

'What do you want?' she asked through gritted teeth when she opened the door and saw him standing there. He looked devastating in a grey suede jacket and white silk shirt, but she hardened her heart.

His jaw tensed and his nostrils dilated as they always did when he was angry. 'You should know why. I've come to take you out.'

'I told you I wouldn't come,' she said shortly, wishing her pulses would stop racing.

'But I insist. I'll wait while you get ready.'

He already had one foot inside when she slammed the door at him. 'There's no point, Kiel. I have no intention of changing my mind.'

'Then I'll change it for you.' With effortless ease he forced the door open again.

'Correct me if I'm wrong,' she said icily, 'but I seem to remember you once saying that you never forced yourself on anyone.'

'This is different.'

'How different?' she objected. 'You're destroying my life, Kiel Kramer. Am I supposed to put up with that? Just go, will you? I have no wish to see you or have anything to do with you other than at the office. And you're making my life so unbearable I might even give that up. Now are you happy? Isn't that what you want?'

Suddenly, and without warning, he pushed her out of the way and marched inside. Tamara had no recourse but to follow. 'How dare you?' she yelled. 'Get out of my house!'

In the sitting-room he swung round to face her, his body rigid, his face a mask of anger and hurt and a whole host of other unreadable emotions. 'That's rich, claiming I'm trying to destroy your life. Don't you think you destroyed mine when you killed Anna?'

'*I* killed her? *I* killed her?' Tamara glared at him, her breathing erratic, her anger suddenly getting the better of her. 'Perhaps it's time you knew the truth.'

His eyes narrowed until they were mere silver slits. 'What the hell are you talking about?'

For just an instant Tamara wondered whether she ought to stop now before it was too late. Did she really want to shatter the image he treasured of his sister?

'Dammit, Tamara, tell me.' His hands were on her shoulders, shaking her, bruising, hurting. 'What have you been hiding?'

She swallowed hard and tried to regain her dignity. 'Let go of me and I'll tell you.'

With obvious reluctance he did so, but he was still standing so close that she could not think clearly. She backed to the door and leaned against it. He watched her closely, not for one instant taking his eyes off her face.

'Anna—Anna wasn't quite the innocent you thought,' she began hesitantly, stopping when he roared his disbelief.

'Hell, I don't want to hear any of these lies. Why are you doing this? What are you trying to prove?'

'It's true, Kiel,' she said quietly. 'As Anna grew up she resented the way you were always trying to protect her.'

He roared again. 'What I did was for her own good. Anna was a frail child, you know that, she needed looking after.'

'She felt stifled,' continued Tamara, swallowing hard, wishing she hadn't started. She ought to have known he wouldn't believe her. 'You were over-protective. She wasn't free to live her own life. Always you wanted to know exactly what she was doing, where she was going, who with, what time she would be back, and if she dared to be a minute late you let rip.'

His chin lifted, his eyes sceptical. 'I was her mother and father rolled into one. I had to look after her. She actually told you this?' he questioned harshly.

'Anna was my closest friend. Girls talk.'

'And so, what are you trying to tell me now?' He still looked as though he doubted the truth of her words.

'She began lying to you about where she was going.'

A growl of incredulity.

'She got in with the wrong crowd.'

A groan.

'On the night she died *she* asked me to go to the party with her. Not the other way round. I didn't know it was a drugs party until we got there. By the time I'd realised what was happening Anna was already high. I dragged her out, she hated me for it, she fought me like a wild-cat. I managed to get her into the car but she was still fighting, she pulled the wheel——' Tamara's voice broke as she relived the moment. 'And the rest you know.'

Silence, absolute silence. Every vestige of colour drained out of his face. He stood looking at her, not wanting to believe it but knowing he must. In the end he sat down, he looked ten years older, and Tamara began to cry. Slow tears at first, and then they raced down her cheeks and dripped off the end of her nose. Tears for Anna. Tears for the illusion Kiel had carried around all these years.

She looked at him and his head was bowed; she wondered whether he was crying too. It was an awful thing for him to discover. He had loved Anna so much. Her throat was a tight knot of emotion and silently she left the room. Kiel needed some time alone with his grief.

In the kitchen she filled the kettle and put it on to boil. She reached out the teapot and cups and then stood and waited.

Suddenly a roar came from the other room. *'Tamara!'*

His angry tone startled her.

'Tamara!' He charged into the kitchen like an enraged bull. 'What right did you have to withhold that information?'

Her eyes widened in astonishment. 'I thought that——'

'You thought what?' he sneered. 'Surely you weren't trying to protect me? Don't you think I would have preferred to know the truth? What right had you to play God?'

Tamara closed her eyes and turned her back on him. She ought to have known that he would turn the tables, that he would still make out it was all her fault.

'Look at me, damn you.'

Slowly she turned around, her eyes blank. 'I did it for you, Kiel. To preserve your illusions about your sister. You loved her so much I didn't think you'd want to know what she was doing.'

'Since when have you cared about what I feel?' he jeered.

Tamara met the platinum coldness in his eyes and something inside her snapped. She picked up a teacup and hurled it at him. 'You monster! Simply because you don't have any feelings, it doesn't mean other people are the same. I thought I was doing the right thing. Obviously not. You condemned me when you thought the accident was my fault, and you're condemning me now you know it wasn't.' She looked at the smashed cup, which he had easily side-stepped, and she looked at his raw, hurt face. 'You'd do us both a favour if you left.'

Their eyes locked and warred for what seemed like a lifetime, before finally, with anger still emanating from every line of his body, Kiel strode from the room.

CHAPTER EIGHT

SEVERAL long, silent minutes went by before Tamara moved. She regretted the burst of anger that had made her spill out the truth, yet it was a relief after all these years. Kiel would never again be able to blame her for Anna's death.

The more she thought about it, the more pleased she was that she had told him. It could, after all, turn out for the best. Kiel might now see her in a different light. It could make a world of difference to their relationship.

She grew excited at the thought, but the next day Kiel did not move out of his office. Tamara kept well clear, guessing he was having difficulty in coming to terms with the fact that his sister had not been the innocent child he'd thought her. He was finding it hard to accept that she had rebelled against his authority. He had always thought he had been doing the right thing. It would take him time to adjust. But soon, she thought, soon, everything will be all right.

The meeting with Princess Margherita was scheduled for Friday afternoon and Tamara went to work in a black velvet suit beneath which she wore a black and gold Paisley satin blouse. She brushed her hair severely back off her face, fixing it in an elaborate coil at her nape, and fastened heavy jet earrings of her own design to her ears. The result, she hoped, was one of cool efficiency.

They were taking the inter-city express from New Street station, and in the taxi on the way Kiel's face was grim, more so than usual. Surely, she thought, he wasn't still dwelling on what had happened to his sister? Not after four whole days?

The journey took only a few minutes and the train was pulling into the station when they got there. Once seated, Kiel reached for his newspaper and it was a full three quarters of an hour before he folded it and put it back into his briefcase.

Tamara knew she had to say something. 'How long is this going on?'

He frowned harshly and looked at her, and as their eyes met Tamara felt the familiar swimming of her senses. 'I don't know what you're talking about,' he said brusquely.

'This affair about Anna—how long are you going to cut me dead because I didn't tell you what had really happened? I thought it would make a difference to us. What a fool I was. But it's a ridiculous state of affairs. This meeting with Princess Margherita will be impossible if there's an atmosphere between us.'

'If it's worrying you, then I suggest you do something about it.' His eyes glittered with reptilian coldness.

Tamara looked at him sharply. 'What's that supposed to mean? You've erected a barrier that no words can penetrate.'

'And you find that difficult to understand?'

'Yes, as a matter of fact, I do,' she answered sharply. 'You could at least make an effort. This order is important to us, or don't you care any more? Are you going to let the business go down and down until it's not worth saving?'

'The hell I am,' he crisped. 'I'm as devastated as you by what's happening. But this is something more personal.'

'You're telling me,' she flung back, heedless of heads being turned in their direction. 'But if it affects business I think something should be done about it.'

'I think you should have told me before about Anna.'

'I don't think I should have told you at all,' Tamara said firmly. 'It's ruined what little bit of respect we had for each other.'

He did not deny it. 'But you're right,' he said, 'we can't afford to lose this commission. I declare a truce for the rest of the day.'

She frowned, but he looked perfectly serious, though there was something in his eyes that she could not quite fathom. When he held out his hand she put hers into it, fighting the sudden surge of sensation that shot through her.

The rest of the journey passed in comparative peace. She voiced her fears that Princess Margherita might not like her designs and Kiel reassured her that they were stunning and the woman could not help liking them.

The Princess and her entourage had taken over the whole top floor of the hotel, and Tamara and Kiel were shown into an elegant pink and gold room. Shortly afterwards Princess Margherita entered. She was even more beautiful than in her pictures, with a warm, pleasant personality, and she put Tamara immediately at her ease.

The designs were produced and the Princess enthused over them. They were prefect, exactly what she wanted, how clever they were, and how soon could they be made? She would like to wear them for a ball she was attending in a little over a month's time. Would they be ready for then?

When they left Tamara felt as though she were walking on air. She gave a little skip of sheer happiness and wanted to fling her arms around Kiel, but knew she did not dare. Instead she gave him a brilliant smile. 'What do you think? Isn't it fantastic? She likes them. She loves them. What a boost this will be for Wilding Jewellery.'

'I never doubted it for one minute.' He grinned, obviously well pleased too, no trace at all now of his earlier aloofness. 'There's no better designer than you, and there's no saying where this might lead once word gets around. I think we should celebrate.'

'But of course.' Tamara smiled, willing to agree to anything while he was in this mood.

'I think we should stay in London the night, have a meal fit for a king and drink champagne until it's running out of our ears.'

Tamara instantly sobered. 'I don't know about that.'

'Scared?' he mocked.

'Of course not,' she answered evenly, 'but I haven't come prepared for an overnight stay.'

'That can easily be remedied. We'll go shopping.'

He made it sound simple and exciting, but she didn't trust him. And if he plied her with champagne, which she loved but which always went to her head, there was no saying what she might do.

'Tamara, I'm waiting.'

Slowly she nodded, knowing she might regret it later but seeming to have no mind of her own. Kiel in this mood was impossible to resist.

He looked pleased and they shopped in Bond Street for lingerie and nightwear, for a new shirt for Kiel and a dress for Tamara, and he insisted on paying. Their arms laden with parcels, he hailed a passing taxi, and Tamara did not hear his directions but when they arrived at the Selfridge and were obviously expected she knew this was no spur of the moment decision.

'You had all this arranged!' she accused, her eyes flashing with sudden anger.

'Just in case,' he agreed easily, not in the least perturbed by her sharp words.

'What if we'd lost the order?' she protested. 'What if I hadn't agreed?'

'I knew we'd get it and I knew you would.' His black mood had completely disappeared. He seemed almost boyish because he had played a trick on her and succeeded.

Their parcels were carried for them and they were shown to their rooms, and if anyone thought it odd that they had no proper luggage they were too discreet to raise so much as an eyebrow.

Tamara stripped off her clothes and took a shower, then she threw herself down on the bed and fell asleep. The next thing she knew Kiel was thumping on her door.

'Tamara, are you ready?'

She dragged herself awake with difficulty, pulling the bath towel around her, wondering what time it was.

'Tamara!' His voice was louder, more insistent.

She walked to the door and called through it. 'I'm sorry, Kiel, I've been to sleep.'

'I have dinner booked for ten minutes' time. You'd best hurry.'

'All right, *all right*,' she said, at the sound of his impatient voice. 'I'll be as quick as I can.'

She pulled on her new, exquisite lace briefs, and the even more beautiful white loosely knitted dress, embroidered with mother-of-pearl sequins. It was sleeveless and backless and had been Kiel's choice. She left her hair loose, though she refused to admit it was to please Kiel—she simply had no time to do anything else.

His room was opposite hers and his door stood open. Tamara paused outside and he beckoned her in, looking at her for a moment, seeing the beautiful woman inside the dress, making his appreciation of her obvious, sending a flurry of awareness through each and every one of her nerves.

When finally she was able to drag her eyes away Tamara was disconcerted to see that a table had been set for two. Candles were already alight, reflecting their flames in the crystal glasses and silver. Heavy damask napkins were folded into stiff water-lilies, and even as she looked a white-coated waiter preceded the dinner-trolley, guiding her to her seat, making sure she was comfortable, shaking out the napkin and laying it on her lap.

She was given no opportunity to object. She had expected nothing like this and she flashed Kiel a disapproving glance. He merely grinned and took his seat opposite.

Once the champagne had been opened and their glasses filled, once the first course had been set in front of them, Kiel dismissed the waiter. Only then did she give vent to her anger. 'You should have consulted me before you arranged something like this,' she snapped. She was, in all truthfulness, a little frightened of this intimate dinner, a little frightened of what might happen afterwards, what he might expect of her. 'I'd have much preferred dinner downstairs.'

'With the safety of other people?' he taunted. 'Forget it, Tamara. Enjoy yourself.' He picked up his glass of champagne. 'A toast I think to Princess Margherita, to the success of the business, and to you also, my beautiful young friend, without whom none of this would have been possible.'

It was an excellent meal and the champagne, as she had known it would do, went straight to her head. She relaxed and they laughed and talked and, after they had finished eating and the trolley had been wheeled away, Kiel slotted in a cassette and asked her whether she would like to dance.

If she had not been drinking Tamara would have refused—she would have known the danger of letting herself be held against him. Instead she floated into his arms and they drifted around the room to the soft strains of somebody's orchestra. She felt as though she were in a dreamlike world.

She could feel the whole, hard length of him, thighs brushing thighs, her breasts crushed, heartbeats hammering. His hands moved sensually over the perfumed skin of her back and her entire body felt as though it were on fire. All animosity was forgotten. She looked up at him, her lips parted, unconsciously pleading to be kissed.

His eyes darkened and he looked at her for one long, questioning moment before his mouth closed on hers. It was a kiss that went on and on, a kiss that threatened her sanity. His mouth moved with insistent urgency, covering every inch of her face, moving with aching slowness down the column of her throat. He undid the single button behind her neck that held her dress in place and the delicate fabric fell obligingly from her naked breasts.

'You're beautiful,' he breathed reverently, his eyes feasting themselves on her. 'Quite, quite beautiful. By far the most feminine woman I've ever met.'

He traced her outline, soft, feather-light touches that set her skin pulsing as though it had been infused by a thousand tiny electric shocks, and made her hunger for more.

She reached out for him, tried to pull him close, but he shook his head and in response lifted her gently into his arms and carried her to the bed.

'Kiel?' There was sudden panic in her voice.

'I'll stop any time you want me to.'

He must have known that it was only a token objection, that she wanted him as much as he wanted her. He laid her down and then began to unbutton his shirt. She watched him with hungry eyes, seeing the tanned hardness of his tightly muscled chest, wanting to touch him, wanting to help him, wishing he would hurry.

His shoes and socks came off next, and then his trousers, and last of all his underpants. He showed no embarrassment as he slid on to the bed beside her, supporting himself on one elbow, reaching out with his other hand and gently touching her face. 'How have I resisted you all this time, my beautiful Tamara?'

She looked back at him with soft brown eyes, swallowing hard, wondering whether she ought to stop him now. But when his hand trailed over her throat and across the soft skin of her shoulders, moving inexorably lower to close over her breast, she knew it was too late.

A gasp of sheer pleasure escaped her, and when his thumb brushed over her erect nipple a shudder of desire ran through her. His mouth was on hers again, more insistent this time, a deeply sensuous exploration that sent fresh rivers of desire shooting through her.

Without seeming to move their bodies were now touching and excitement danced through Tamara's veins. This was the culmination of all her dreams and for the moment it did not matter that emotionally it meant nothing to Kiel.

She returned his kiss with all the depth of feeling he had aroused, her fingers roaming through the coarseness of his hair, feeling and exhilarating in the muscular strength of his shoulders and arms.

At the same time his fingers explored further, touching, inciting, totally experienced, knowing exactly what he was doing to her. They slid beneath the fine silk of her panties, easing them down, Tamara obligingly lifting her body. He raised her to higher peaks of pleasure than she had ever known existed. She was completely sensitised, utterly attuned to him, and a compulsion built in her that she knew had to be fulfilled.

Her whole body trembled in anticipation but he was in no hurry. His assault was slow and deliberate, knowing that when he finally entered her she would be ready for him. She would be as deeply in need of him as he was her.

Tamara had never felt this close to any man before; she had never felt a bond like the one that was drawing her to Kiel. It had been there all her life, buried deep, waiting for the right moment. And this was it. She loved him. Without any shadow of doubt she loved him, and because of that she was ready to let him make love to her. It would be a memory to keep and treasure, to recall in the darker days of her life.

Finally, after what seemed like an eternity of aching, shuddering pleasure, when every one of her senses was aroused to spinning fever pitch, he began to enter her, pausing only briefly when he found that no man had been there before. Tamara lifted her hips to meet him, to urge him, to encourage him, not even wincing at the second's sharp spasm of pain. Then they were one.

Two bodies joined by a mutual hunger, two throbbing, pulsing human beings who had lifted themselves from this planet and were spinning in a world where only senses mattered.

Tamara had never felt so contented, so beautifully at peace, and she regretted only that it was over. When Kiel moved it was as though part of her was being separated, and she put out her hand to stop him. 'Stay with me, Kiel. Stay with me.'

'You've no regrets?' His tone was gentle, with none of the hardness she normally associated with him.

She shook her head, her eyes shining as she looked at Kiel.

'You should have stopped me,' he said.

'I didn't want to.' Her voice was a mere whisper, an aching whisper that told of her emotional disturbance.

'But you should have done.' There was a faint note of accusation now in his tone.

Tamara frowned. 'Are you having regrets? Is that what you're trying to tell me?'

'You're damn right I am.' He jerked himself suddenly upright, startling her, causing her eyes to widen with surprise. 'I must have been out of my mind.'

Tamara shook her head in despair and disbelief, all the beautiful, warm feelings abruptly draining out of her. What had happened to him? She swung herself over to the other side of the bed and sat on the edge, pulling the sheet around her, feeling embarrassed now by her nudity. 'I don't understand. I explained about Anna. You can't go on blaming me.'

'Forget Anna,' he snarled. 'It's now, it's us that counts. Why didn't you tell me that you were a virgin?'

Tamara closed her eyes in relief. Was that all that was worrying him? 'It's not important. What is important is that—— '

'To me it matters,' he cut in abruptly. 'Why didn't you stop me?'

'Why?' she echoed. 'I didn't stop you, Kiel, because I wanted you to make love to me, and I thought you wanted it too. But if it bothers you that much why didn't *you* stop? Why lay the blame on me?'

The breath hissed slowly out of him. 'Can you stop the rain falling? Can you stop the sun shining? I'm only human, Tamara.'

Her lips twisted bitterly. 'Anyone halfway towards being human wouldn't make such a fuss.'

'You don't understand.'

'What I do know,' she retorted, 'is that you had this whole thing planned all along.'

'No, Tamara.' He grimaced. 'The rooms, yes. I fully intended staying the night here. But the bed, no. *No!*'

'You expect me to believe that?' Scepticism flared in her eyes. 'You've made no secret lately of the fact that you want to make love to me. What's wrong? Wasn't it as good as you thought? Did I disappoint you? Am I not experienced enough?' She snatched up her dress and her shoes and, still with the sheet clutched tightly about her, she left the room, thankful there was no one in the corridor to see her undignified exit. It took all her self-control not to break down in tears. She tried telling herself that he was a swine and she hated him, but it did not work. She loved Kiel.

The emotion had crept up on her without her knowing it. But it was unlikely he would ever touch her again.

Sleep had never been more difficult. She lay and listened to the traffic in the street outside, her body reliving every single, mind-shattering moment of Kiel's lovemaking, even down to the fact that he had ultimately destroyed it like a snail crushed beneath his heel.

Her fingers curled every time she reached this point, nails digging into her palms, her fists thumping the bed at her side. She couldn't believe that Kiel could be so moral, that it mattered so much to him. It was probably a get-out. He had achieved what he had been planning for a long time and now he wanted nothing more to do with her. She held her body so rigid that it ached and she woke the next morning feeling that she hadn't slept at all.

Tamara thought Kiel might have come to terms with himself during the night, but it was not the case. At breakfast he barely spoke to her, lost in a world of his own, and the train journey was long, silent and uncomfortable. She had never been more thankful to get home.

Sunday she spent going back over the events of the weekend, and still she could not understand Kiel's reaction. She had really thought that at last, now he knew the truth about Anna, they were getting their act together. She had been so happy, so very much in love. Instead he had proved beyond any shadow of doubt that this would never be the case, and she felt more lonely and insulted than ever in her life.

Work on the Princess's necklace and earrings began and there was great excitement within the workforce. Tamara was also infected by it. These were by far the most important pieces of work they had ever been asked to make.

Bill and Paul, as the most senior employees, were doing most of the work, though everyone did something. They all wanted to say that they'd had a hand in making Princess Margherita's jewellery.

But undermining the excitement was the fact that business was still dropping off. Still more orders were cancelled and fewer enquiries came in. Tamara kept trying to tell herself that it was no longer her concern, but she couldn't forget the fact that her father had built the business up from scratch. It wouldn't have been natural for her not to feel something, so finally she marched into Kiel's office demanding to know what he was doing about it.

'The business is going down the drain. Don't you care?' She refused to see the lines of strain on his face, the fatigue behind his eyes. They were of his own making.

He looked at her coldly. 'You think I'm not in love with this firm as much as Ben was?'

'All I know is that you're sitting on your backside and doing precious sweet nothing about it,' she flashed.

He glanced at her coldly. 'I might have known you'd think that.'

'Then tell me what you are doing!' She marched to his desk and put her hands down on it, furiously meeting the stormy grey of his eyes.

'I prefer to say nothing at this stage.'

'Because you're doing nothing,' she accused sharply.

'Because I have my own reasons.' His voice was quiet, too quiet, warning her that she was treading on dangerous ground. He stood up and now Tamara had to lift her chin to look into his eyes. Her advantage had gone.

'Do you honestly believe,' he asked, coming round the desk to stand in front of her, 'that I would sit back and let the business slide? That I am not trying to discover how the wrong gems were used, and that I'm not trying to convince our customers that it was all an unfortunate mistake and will never happen again?'

'If you are you don't seem to be making much headway,' she flung crossly. 'Orders are still being cancelled.'

'To my intense disappointment,' he snarled, 'but we'll get over it. Once word gets around that we've made specially commissioned pieces of jewellery for royalty our name will take on a new meaning.'

'And you're waiting for that, are you?' she scorned.

'Hell, Tamara.' His voice rose in an angry roar. 'I'm as worried as you, more so probably, and I don't need you adding to it.'

Tamara found it difficult to believe that there had ever been any tender moments between them, that she had lain in his arms and he had made love to her, that she had felt as though she were his most precious possession. He was looking at her now as though she were an insect who had crawled out of the woodwork. His face was paler than she had ever seen it, his fingers clenching and unclenching at his sides.

'If my father were alive he'd have done something by now,' she told him coldly and furiously. 'As a matter of fact if he'd been alive this would never have happened.'

His eyes narrowed and became dangerous. 'You're blaming me?'

'Who else is there to blame?' she demanded. 'You and Samantha are the newcomers. You're the obvious suspects.'

'Get out, Tamara!' The words were quietly spoken, but his mouth was grim, his eyes icy.

'You don't like the truth?' she asked caustically.

'I don't like people who cast aspersion. You have no proof that Samantha is involved.'

'Then you tell me why these switches have only happened since she started here?'

He sighed heavily. 'I don't know, Tamara. I wish I did. But one day soon I will have the answer, I can assure you of that.'

'I hope you're right,' she said bitterly. 'Wilding Jewellery can't afford any more mistakes. I know it's wrong of me to worry now that it belongs to you, but I still feel a part of it. I guess I always will. Maybe I should leave after all?'

A momentary flicker in his eyes, then blankness. 'I guess that's up to you.'

Tamara's heart felt heavy. She had hoped Kiel would tell her not to be silly, but obviously he didn't care a fig whether she stayed or left. She meant nothing to him at all, absolutely nothing.

In the days that followed Kiel and Samantha were once again bosom friends. They had clearly worked out their differences, and Tamara's green eye of jealousy had never been stronger. She wondered what the girl would say if she knew Kiel had made love to her? What a smack in the eye that would be.

She couldn't really weigh up Kiel's feelings towards this other girl. He affected indifference and yet he was spending so much time with her. Did the fact that Samantha was keen make up for it? Was she the woman he needed to feed his male ego? Did he have no hang-ups about making love to her?

And still the decline of the business weighed heavily on Tamara's mind. Every day she went through the books. Every day the situation depressed her. Even though the cancellations seemed to have stopped, no new orders were coming in. She found herself with less and less to do, and more time to worry about it, and to think about Kiel, and her love for him, and his indifference towards her. It was never-ending.

Patti paid one of her infrequent visits and exclaimed when she saw her friend's pale face. 'What on earth's the matter, Tammy? Are you ill? Are you still grieving over your father?'

Tamara shook her head. 'I'm worried about the business—it isn't doing very well.'

'I'm surprised,' said Patti. 'I thought Kiel was good? But surely it's nothing to do with you any more?'

'I can't help it,' admitted Tamara bitterly. 'It's inbred. I'm actually glad my father's not here to see what's happening. It would break his heart after all the years of hard work he's put in.'

'But there must be a reason.' Patti frowned.

'Oh, there is, a very big one. A couple of cases of fraud that have only happened since Samantha came on the scene.'

Patti whistled, her green eyes widening in shocked horror. 'Is that true?'

Tamara nodded.

'My goodness. What's Kiel done about it?'

'Not a thing. He's looking into it, he says. If you ask me he's dragging his feet.'

'Because he loves the girl?'

Patti had put into words something Tamara had refused to consider. But it actually seemed the only logical explanation. 'I don't know,' she said wearily.

'So he hasn't involved the police?'

'Not yet.'

'Then I think you should. I think in a case like this you should go over the top of his head.'

'If anything else happens, anything at all, then I shan't hesitate,' she announced firmly.

'Atta girl,' said Patti, grinning. 'Now can I tell you my good news?'

'I'm sorry, of course.' Tamara noticed for the first time how radiant her friend was.

'I'm getting married.'

Tamara's face lit up. 'That's wonderful. When?'

'In September, and I want you, Tamara, to be my bridesmaid.'

'I'd have been upset if you hadn't asked. Oh, Patti.' She hugged her friend. 'I'm so pleased for you. Rory's a fantastic guy.'

'I think so,' said Patti. 'I wish everyone were as happy as I am. I wish you and Kiel would make a go of things. We could have a double wedding. He's perfect for you, you know.'

'Try telling him that,' said Tamara drily, and quickly changed the subject.

When the day finally came that the Princess's jewellery was finished and dispatched, Kiel came into her office. For the first time in ages his face had lost its worried expression and he was smiling. 'I think this calls for another celebration. I'll take you out for a meal.'

Tamara frowned, recalling the last occasion, and shook her head. 'No, thanks, I don't think so. We could have a drink here if you like?'

'I insist, Tamara.' His grey eyes were fixed firmly on hers, hypnotising her. 'You still look as though you aren't eating properly.'

And so did he! 'It wouldn't work,' she said flatly, trying to look away but finding it impossible.

A flash of anger darkened his eyes. 'I have no intention of taking no for an answer. I'll pick you up at eight.'

'You'll be wasting your time.'

'Make sure you're ready.' His eyes held hers for a few seconds more before he swung on his heel. 'I mean it, Tamara,' he said from the door.

And she had meant it when she had said she wasn't going out with him. If he turned up he would find an empty house. He wasn't going to hurt and humiliate her again.

There was a film showing that she particularly wanted to see. She would go tonight; she would leave the house long before Kiel put in an appearance. But when she opened her front door ready to go his car was in the drive and he was just getting out. 'Going somewhere?'

Tamara groaned inwardly, while at the same time her traitorous body recognised his overt sexuality, re-lived those dangerous moments of togetherness. 'I told you I didn't want to go out with you,' she said sharply.

'So you thought you'd disappear before I arrived?' He actually had the nerve to look amused.

'You're early!'

'Because I suspected you might try something like this. Jump in, Tamara, let's go.'

She was left with no alternative, but as she slid into his red Mercedes she could not help wondering why he was being so insistent, and she was determined not to enjoy herself, not to let her love for him show.

CHAPTER NINE

FEELINGS Tamara had done her best to suppress over the last few days and weeks sprang back into life when she was sitting beside Kiel. It was going to be a difficult evening and she wished she knew why he had suggested it. She found it hard to believe that it was simply to toast the success of the Princess's jewels.

The place he took her to was a whole new experience. They headed out of the city and her first impression was of a country pub serving bar meals, which suited her perfectly because she wasn't dressed for a fashionable restaurant. But at the back of the building, reached by a covered walkway, were two Pullman railway coaches, restored to their original nineteenth-century splendour with velvet curtains and gas lamps, with padded seats and ornate mirrors.

'This is beautiful,' said Tamara in surprise, smiling, relaxing suddenly. But her heart dropped when they were shown into a compartment that had its own door and effectively shut them off from the rest of the diners.

It would have been perfect if things had been different between them, if Kiel had loved her too. It was a place for lovers, a place to be alone in, completely alone, to talk and express feelings and emotions without anyone intruding or overhearing.

'Do you like it?'

She slid into her seat and nodded. 'Well, yes, I do, but it's a little—intimate, don't you think?'

He frowned. 'That bothers you?'

How could she say yes after the intimacies they had shared? When their two bodies had merged as one and it had been the most beautiful experience of her life? The only way to hide the torture of loving him was in anger. 'Of course it bothers me,' she said bitterly, 'after what happened the last time.'

'I simply want this to be an evening to remember.'

Her eyes flashed. 'Why?' There was only one evening that would stay with her for the rest of her life.

'Because it's a turning-point.'

'Really? I don't see how one special order can restore our customers' confidence,' she said coldly. And yet one night out with him was turning her stomach into a mass of sensation. She ought not to have come. She ought not to have let him bully her into it.

'It can lead to new business,' he insisted.

She snorted derisively. 'If you're relying on that then you're a fool. You should be thinking about repairing the damage that has already been done.'

'Believe me, I'm working on it.'

Tamara did not believe him and it was obvious in her eyes.

He snorted his impatience. 'You're determined to ruin the evening before it's even begun, aren't you? What would you like to drink?'

'A tomato juice, please.'

A brow rose but he made no comment, though his jaw was tense as he gave their order. Tamara made a pretence of studying the menu, but all the time she was conscious of Kiel's eyes on her, and much as she tried to fight the feelings he evoked she found it impossible. He could not be ignored. Even in the midst of anger and confusion, and every other emotion she was experiencing, her body craved fulfilment.

There was very little space in the compartment, the table was narrow, their knees almost touching and his presence overpowering. She breathed him in, almost tasted him, conscious of every movement he made, of the aching pleasure that pulsed through her.

She drank her tomato juice, she ate her meal, she sipped a glass of wine, she answered when he spoke to her, but she did all these things automatically, almost without being aware of it. She was aware only of Kiel and she was glad when the meal came to an end, when they could escape the tiny compartment that had become a prison.

He drove her home and there was silence between them, but it was silence of a different kind. She wanted to reach out and touch him, to break his self-imposed virtue, but she did not dare. She was afraid of what it might lead to.

When she fetched her key out of her bag he took it from her and turned it in the lock, standing back for her to enter and then following her inside.

'There's no need,' said Tamara at once, panic in her voice.

He frowned harshly. 'You know I don't like you coming into an empty house alone.'

'I've done it ever since my mother went away,' she told him firmly, but it made no difference. He shut the door behind them and followed her into the living-room.

'Has Hilary said anything more about moving in with her sister permanently?' he asked.

'She's still thinking about it,' answered Tamara. 'Would you like a cup of coffee?' She did not really want to encourage him, but he had already taken off his jacket and settled into a corner of the settee. He looked ready to stay for a long time.

'Not yet,' he answered. 'Sit down and relax.'

Tamara knew that would be impossible. Nevertheless she perched on the edge of an armchair and looked at him. 'I wish I knew why you really wanted to see me tonight, Kiel. I can't believe that it's simply to celebrate the fact that Princess Margherita's jewellery is finished.'

'Why do you find that so hard to believe?'

'Because we've not exactly been friends these last few weeks.'

'My fault,' he admitted, much to her surprise. 'I think it's time that was remedied if we're to pull the company back together. I need you on my side, Tamara, as much as you need me. I cannot take the risk of your leaving.'

So that was it! Tamara stood up and pretended to rearrange a figurine on the sideboard. She ought to have known that there was nothing personal in it. There would be no more designs on her body. The only designs he was interested in were pieces of jewellery.

Tears pricked the backs of her eyelids, but she refused to give in and let him see that he had hurt her. 'I won't leave,' she said softly, almost painfully.

'Good. I think I will have that cup of coffee now.'

To her relief he did not follow her into the kitchen, and afterwards they sat and talked and she told him how even as a child she had designed jewellery. She had wound wire around her finger and threaded a daisy on it and thought it the most wonderful ring in the world.

But it was hard talking like this when her body was telling stories of a different kind. It was a relief when he went.

During the next few days they got on better than they had in a long while. There were no intimacies, no hint of sexuality at all in his attitude, and Tamara knew it was for the best. She was coping. She knew where she stood and that meant a lot.

But then came a phone call that devastated her. It was for Kiel, but as he was out she took it in his place, and was told that two of the diamonds in the Princess's necklace weren't diamonds at all. They were zircons.

Her heart missed a beat. It just wasn't possible. She had studied the necklace herself before it had gone out, and had seen nothing wrong. Whoever had done it had been very cunning. Where the design curved, where the light did not hit the diamonds with the same brilliance, those were the stones that had been replaced.

She felt as though her world were crashing about her shoulders. She could not believe it. And this time she had no doubt that Samantha was the culprit. Samantha had set some of the stones and Tamara was prepared to bet everything she owned that they were the ones that were in dispute.

She picked up the phone and rang the police.

When Kiel came back a few minutes later he was furious when he found out what Tamara had done. 'Why didn't you consult me first?' His eyes flashed a savage silver beneath jutting, angular brows. 'Why did you do it?'

'Why? You ask me why? Isn't it obvious? It's because I didn't want you saying again that you'd sort it out yourself. This could ruin the company altogether, Kiel. Don't you see that?' There was blazing fury in her own eyes as well now. 'Don't you care? It was the worst thing my father ever did when he left it to you.'

'I might have known you'd say that.' Kiel's jaw was tight, muscles jerking spasmodically, his fingers clenched into tight fists. 'But let me——'

'I know what you're doing,' she cut in, her voice beginning to rise hysterically. 'You're protecting Samantha. She's the culprit, isn't she? She's the one who's doing all this. But because you're so infatuated with her you're prepared to sit back and let it fall to pieces around your head.'

'Tamara, listen, I——'

'No, Kiel, you listen to me. I put as much hard work into this company as my father did and I'm not going to let you ruin it. I should have followed my instincts the first time and done something about it. I should have called the police then, I should have——'

Kiel's angry exclamation silenced her and as she glared at him two huge tears rolled down her cheeks. At that moment the police arrived.

Statements were taken, every member of the staff interviewed individually, including herself and Kiel. It took the whole day. And when Tamara went home that night she cried herself to sleep.

She dreamt about Kiel, a dream that was totally different from the truth. An erotic dream where they made gentle and tender love. He was everything she could wish for, he was interested in nothing but her, he loved her. He told her over and over again, and she awoke with a smile on her lips and a warm glow inside her.

But it did not last long. Reality asserted itself, and he called her into his office the moment she arrived.

He looked as though he hadn't slept a wink. His face was all grim, taut lines, his jaw aggressive.

'Have the police come up with anything?' she asked him.

'Not yet.'

'Is something else wrong?' She did not like the cold glitter in his eyes.

'There's a lot wrong,' he said sharply.

'Has the news leaked out already?'

'I'm talking about you and me,' he rasped.

'I don't suppose there's ever been anything right with you and me,' she said quickly. 'We've been at odds all our lives, more so since Anna died.'

'You're the most infuriating female I've ever met. You don't give a damn about whose feelings you hurt.'

'If you're talking about Samantha then prove to me that you aren't shielding her and I'll gladly apologise,' she said.

He snorted angrily. 'You said to me once, Tamara, that there was only room for one of us here, and I'm beginning to think that you're right.'

He was giving her the sack! Tamara swallowed hard. It wasn't enough that Samantha was setting out to ruin them—he was getting rid of her as well. She fought back bitter tears as she thought of all the years of hard work her father had put into making Wilding Jewellery a top-class firm with one of the highest reputations around.

'When this thing's over, when the police find out who's been switching the stones, then it will be the end of the road for us.'

She stood and blindly looked at him, finding it difficult to believe that he was doing this to her. Her father had been dead only a few weeks—and now this!

'I'll get out. You'll never see me again. You can have the company, lock, stock and barrel.'

Tamara could not believe what she was hearing. It made nonsense of everything that she had thought. Her eyes widened as she looked at him in stunned disbelief.

'What's wrong?' he sneered. 'Isn't that what you wanted?'

Oh, lord, she didn't know what she wanted. But she had certainly never expected this. Kiel wasn't the type to give in. 'You can't do that.'

'Can't I? Well, you'd better believe it because it's what's going to happen.'

'But you've always wanted this company more than anything else.'

'No, there's something I wanted more.' His mouth twisted bitterly. 'But as there's no chance of that I'm getting out.'

'It should be me who leaves. My father obviously thought you would do a better job running it than I.'

'Ben didn't believe in women doing what he thought were men's jobs. He would never have set Sam on either.'

'Which was your biggest mistake,' she could not help retorting. But she felt bad about his leaving. It wasn't right. And to actually say that he would give her the company, not ask for anything for it, made her feel very humble and small. She couldn't let him do it.

'Kiel, we have to talk about this. I know I didn't agree with what my father did, but he trusted you and he wanted you to have it. You can't walk out.'

'I can and I am,' he told her firmly. 'The subject is closed.'

Tamara was devastated and her mind whirled, but it was equally obvious there was nothing she could say or do to make him change his mind. But a future without Kiel? It was a very bleak prospect.

After work she phoned her mother for their usual chat, though she did not tell her what was going on, and later a reporter turned up on her doorstep. She wondered how he had found out about Princess Margherita's jewels, but she told him nothing either.

Nevertheless it was in the *Birmingham Post* the next evening and Tamara knew that their hard-earned reputation had gone.

A couple of days later she saw Yves again. She had gone into the city during her lunch hour intending to buy a new dress. It was even more difficult working with Kiel now—he spoke to her only when necessary, and she thought something new might cheer her up.

She saw the Frenchman coming out of a restaurant and quickly crossed over the road so that they would not meet. When she risked another glance she saw that he was not alone—he was with, of all people, Paul, their setter.

It was quite a shock—she had not realised that they knew each other—yet they were deep in earnest conversation and she could have walked straight past them and they would not have noticed.

As she had known would happen, business began to fall again and Kiel's efforts to pull it back together were in vain. It looked like the end of the road for her as well as him, she thought despondently.

Tamara lost even more weight with the sheer worry of it all. She hardly ate and slept little and the police seemed no nearer to solving their problem. The Princess's commission was cancelled altogether; she did not want a replacement. Her faith in them had been shattered. This, as far as Tamara was concerned, was the most cruel blow of all, and she was glad her father was not alive to witness it.

When she heard the news she went in to see Kiel. Expressionless grey eyes stared back at her.

'This is the end,' she said. 'There'll be no business left for either of us. At least not the sort we're used to. And I have no intention of making cheap stuff for the chains. I'd rather close down.'

'Is that the Wilding fighting spirit?' he scoffed. 'I'm sure once you've got me out of your hair you'll pull out all the stops and bring the business back to its former glory.'

She met the stony hardness of his eyes but could not hold his gaze, and looked out of the window down into the workshop. Most of the men were standing around doing nothing. Business was so bad the decision would soon have to be made whether to make some of them redundant.

Samantha would be one of the first to go—if the police did not arrest her first! She and Kiel were still as thick as thieves, talking constantly, and it made Tamara sick every time she saw them.

Then her eye fell on Paul. He stood apart from the other men and he was watching Samantha, who was the only one of them working. His face was tight, his eyes hostile, and she recalled the day she had seen him with Yves.

She spoke almost without thinking. 'Did you know that Paul is friendly with Yves?'

Something flashed across Kiel's face then was gone. 'Who told you that?'

'I saw them.'

'When? Where?' His tone was sharp, almost as though he didn't believe her, or didn't want to believe her.

'A few days ago in the city centre. I think they had lunch together.'

'Excuse me, Tamara, I have to go out.' He pushed himself abruptly up from his chair and shrugged on his jacket. She watched as he hurried down the steps and walked swiftly across the workshop floor, pausing only to say a few words to Samantha, and she wondered where he was going in such a hurry.

But the subject was not mentioned again until a few days later when he called her into his office. 'Paul and Yves have been arrested.'

Tamara gasped. 'Paul? Paul and Yves?'

Kiel nodded grimly. 'Yves has had it in for me ever since we were at Cambridge together and I took his girlfriend off him.'

Tamara frowned. 'Is that surprising?'

'He never liked the fact that I was more successful than he, but when I stole Marie from him it was the last straw as far as he was concerned and he always swore to get his own back. I didn't love the girl, or anything like that, you understand. Yves was, to put it mildly, abusing her. She was grateful to me, but that's all there was to it—although he never knew that.'

'So when he discovered you had a company of your own he set out to ruin you?' asked Tamara.

'That's right.'

'So how did Paul get involved? I never thought of him as being the criminal type.'

'He's not, but as you know he hasn't been happy recently because he felt he was being demoted in favour of Sam. And when Yves hung around questioning the workers he found out about Paul's dissatisfaction. It was easy to persuade him to help. Except that Paul didn't realise exactly how far Yves was prepared to go. He's very sorry for what he did.'

Not as sorry as she was. Between them Paul and Yves had succeeded in ruining the company. For a moment Tamara stood in silence, digesting this unexpected piece of information.

'Paul wasn't Yves' first choice.'

She frowned. 'So who was?'

'You!'

Her eyes widened, her hands went to her mouth. 'Me? That's impossible. We never spoke about anything like that. And if he thought I'd try to ruin my father's—your company, then he was crazy.'

'You really upset him when you rejected his advances. He thought he had his revenge beautifully worked out, stealing my girl—I don't know where he got that idea—and ruining my company at the same time.'

'This is incredible.' Tamara shook her head, still unable to take it all in. 'How did you find out?'

'Sam had her suspicions about Paul, but we couldn't prove anything, until you said you'd seen him with Yves. Then it all fell into place. I went to see Yves and tricked him into admitting it. Then I went to the police.'

Tamara swallowed hard. 'I don't know what to say.' She had made a complete fool of herself accusing Samantha.

'Try thank you,' he said icily.

She swallowed hard. 'Thank you, Kiel.'

'And just for the record, I set Sam on because I owed her a favour, nothing more. Her father got me my first job.'

'I see,' said Tamara quietly.

'And now I'm going.'

Suddenly she realised that his desk was clear of its usual clutter. The photo of Anna and his parents had gone. There was nothing at all in the room to remind her of him—except for the ghastly furniture.

He picked up his case and his jacket and he did not even look at her. 'It's all yours, Tamara. Good luck.'

'Kiel, please, wait!'

He turned at the door and looked at her coldly. 'What for? We both know it would never work out. Too much has happened. Your father made a mistake thinking it would help if we were forced together. Goodbye, Tamara.'

'But——'

The door slammed shut. Tamara stood for a whole minute before she walked to his desk and sat in his grey tweed chair. Her chair now. Wasn't this what she wanted? Tears trickled, slowly at first, and then in full flood, her shoulders heaving, her head buried in her hands on the desk.

The full story was reported in the *Birmingham Post* and a short paragraph in most of the national dailies, and gradually business picked up again. Even Princess Margherita's secretary wrote and said that the Princess was sorry she had judged them so harshly and would like the commissioned jewellery to go ahead.

Tamara was busy, busier than she had been in a long time, running the business as well as looking after the design side of things. It was more difficult than she had imagined and she often took work home with her.

Her mother returned and found out about the whole sorry story. She hadn't seen it in the papers and up till now Tamara had deliberately refrained from telling her. 'I wish you'd said something, Tamara. My goodness me, you shouldn't have had to deal with this alone.'

'I didn't want to worry you.'

'But I'm your mother and I love you, and now I wish I weren't moving in with Ida.'

'You've finally made up your mind?'

Hilary Wilding nodded. 'And I'm going to sell this house—it's far too big for you to run. I'll give you half of whatever I get for it and you'll be able to buy yourself a flat or a nice little cottage. It's time you had somewhere of your own. Now tell me about you and Kiel. It's hard to believe that he's gone out of our lives completely. He's always been there. Always. Ever since I met your father.'

'I suppose it was my fault,' confessed Tamara. 'I thought Samantha was the one to blame and I accused him of shielding her—she was in love with him anyway—and he's never forgiven me, Mummy, for Anna's death. It was just a hopeless situation.'

Hilary looked at her daughter sadly. 'You love him, don't you?'

Tamara nodded. She did not know how her mother had guessed, but she was past caring. She had worked and worked since Kiel had left, as much to push him out of her mind as anything else, but she had not succeeded. Always he was there, and she guessed he always would be.

'Then don't you think you should go and see him?'

'No, I don't,' she said at once, horrified at the thought. 'Besides, it wouldn't make any difference—he doesn't love me. But don't worry, I'll get over him.'

'When?' asked her mother sceptically. 'I've never seen you looking so miserable, and you've lost weight. When was the last time you ate a good meal?'

Tamara shrugged. 'I get by.'

During the next two weeks Hilary fussed over Tamara as though she were still a child. She gave her nutritious packed lunches to take to the office and a hot meal awaited her every night when she came home. They talked more than they had ever talked in their lives and meanwhile Mrs Wilding packed all her personal possessions.

The house was put on the market. 'You can have whatever furniture you like and sell the rest,' said Tamara's mother the night before her return to Cheltenham. She wasn't staying to supervise the sale—it would take months, and the house held too many memories. She wanted to get back to her sister.

In the days that followed Tamara grew increasingly sad. This was the beginning of the end of an era. Would-be buyers trooped through the house while she was at work, shown around by the estate agent's representative. She supposed she would have to start to look for a place herself, but somehow she hadn't the heart.

When Kiel appeared at her door one evening with a couple of strangers she thought she was imagining it. He had been on her mind so much that it had to be a hallucination.

He looked every inch as good as she remembered. He was perhaps thinner, his face more gaunt, but he was still the same Kiel she had fallen in love with. And did still love! It broke her heart just looking at him.

He didn't smile; he gave her a curt nod and said, 'I've brought Mr and Mrs Ferenza to look over your house. I trust it's convenient? They unfortunately had to cancel their earlier appointment.'

Tamara frowned. '*You* have brought them. Why?'

'Didn't your mother tell you? I'm handling everything for her. I've tried to make sure that prospective buyers look around while you're not here, but today that was impossible.'

With difficulty Tamara pulled herself together. 'Of course, come in.' Her mother had asked Kiel to look after things! 'I'll make myself scarce.' Why hadn't she said?

Out in the garden Tamara decided it was all part of some diabolical plot on her mother's behalf. A way of bringing her and Kiel together again so that they could iron out their differences. But there was no chance of that. One look at his face told her nothing had changed. And when he left with Mr and Mrs Firenza without speaking to her again she knew it was true.

Each day after that she wondered whether he was inside her house, and when she lay in her bed at night it was with the knowledge that Kiel had been in her room. It was an uncanny feeling, but somehow it drew her closer to him and she knew she could not go on like this forever. They must talk. She would tell him that she loved him and the rest would be up to him.

Her opportunity came when he telephoned to say that a buyer had been found. 'They've already sold their own house and would like the sale to go through as quickly as possible. Have you found anywhere yet?'

'No.' Tamara's heart was banging wildly against her ribcage.

'Then I suggest you do. I have a friend who's selling a flat that might suit you. If you like I can give you his address.'

His tone was distant, as though she were a complete stranger, and Tamara almost got cold feet. But she had to see him. 'Couldn't you take me there yourself?'

A long pause before he finally said, 'I'll give him a ring and if it's convenient I'll pick you up at seven tomorrow.' The phone went dead before she could even thank him.

And at seven on the dot he turned up. Tamara was ready and waiting and she climbed into his Mercedes and immediately felt claustrophobic. It had been a mistake. She couldn't breathe, the whole car was filled with his presence, her whole body responded with a tingling awareness. But he was as coldly indifferent to her as he had ever been. What would be the point in losing her pride?

He did not speak. He did not ask how the business was doing. He remained stonily silent until they reached his friend's flat. Tamara liked it and said she would have it, and then he drove her home.

'Would you like to come in for a cup of coffee?' she asked tentatively, and he would never know the effort it cost her. He had made it plain that he wanted nothing to do with her, the engine was still running, he wanted to get away as soon as possible. 'Please,' she added when he appeared to hesitate. 'I must talk to you.'

'I can't imagine what about,' he said, but he cut the engine and unfolded himself out of the car.

He went into the living-room and Tamara into the kitchen where she made the coffee and took it in to him. He stood at the window looking out at the garden, at the blue swimming-pool which Tamara had not used at all this summer.

He turned when he heard her enter the room and as they sat down his eyes were upon her. Tamara's raw, exposed nerves felt the full impact of his gaze and her hunger for him increased a thousandfold. She loved him, she loved him with every fibre of her being. And now she was going to fight for that love.

She pushed his coffee across the low table towards him, then looked down at her hands and wondered where to begin.

'Go ahead, I'm waiting.' The rough, vibrant tones of his voice made her jump.

'Business is picking up again.' That wasn't what she had meant to say at all, and she was not surprised to hear the cynicism in his voice.

'You must be pleased about that. Is it as good at the top as you imagined?'

'I'm coping.'

'Is that what you wanted to tell me? Did you want to gloat over the fact that you're——'

'No!' cut in Tamara sharply. 'Not that at all. As a matter of fact, I'd welcome you back.'

He frowned sharply.

And that wasn't what she had meant to say either. What was the matter with her? Why couldn't she confess and get it over with?

'Are you offering me the job?'

'No—yes—hell, I don't know. I'm making a mess of this, Kiel. What I wanted to say, firstly, was that I'm sorry I ever hurt you by thinking you were protecting Samantha.'

There was no encouragement in his eyes, nothing except cool indifference, and she went on, 'I resented you, that was the trouble, more than you'll ever know. You had the job that I wanted, that I thought was mine by rights. And then Samantha put in an appearance and I was insanely jealous. Every time I saw you together it was like a knife being turned in my heart.'

Still no emotion on his face. She was baring her soul and it meant nothing. He actually stood up and moved towards the window again, and she had no way of knowing what thoughts were running through his mind.

'It's all right,' she said quickly and loudly, 'you don't have to say anything, you can go. I'm making a fool of myself. I'm sorry.' Fighting back unhappy tears she ran from the room.

She did not hear Kiel follow, she was not aware of him until his hand touched her silently heaving shoulders, then she stood stock-still, but she did not turn and meet his eyes—she was afraid of what she might read there.

'Tamara, there is usually a reason for jealousy.'

Her heart stopped. Did he want her to spell it out? Was he trying to make her humiliation complete? She wished she had never invited him in. It was a mistake, a big mistake. He wanted to throw her love back in her face and finish her completely.

When she took so long in answering he took her silence to mean that he was mistaken and he walked away down the long hall. 'Your apology is accepted, Tamara, I forgive you. I hope your business continues to be a success.'

Tamara was galvanised into action. 'Kiel, wait!' She ran after him. 'Yes, I love you. I love you very much, too much for my own good. I want you and I need you—and these last few weeks have been hell.' Her throat contracted painfully and there were tears in her eyes as she looked proudly at the man she loved. It was all out now and the rest was up to him.

And suddenly the mask of ice that was his face melted, a whole host of emotions flashed through his eyes: disbelief, fear, pain, relief, joy. With an anguished groan he crushed her against him, taking her mouth hungrily, his hands roaming possessively over her body.

Tamara gloried in his touch, arching herself even closer into him, giving herself up to this man whom she had thought lost forever.

'Tamara, my Tamara,' he breathed hoarsely. 'I can't believe what I'm hearing.'

'I've wanted to tell you for so long,' she whispered. 'So very, very long.'

He shook his head, pain and humiliation cutting deep. 'I don't deserve your love.'

Tamara put a finger to his lips. 'Don't say that, Kiel, don't ever say that.'

He kissed her finger gently, then removed it. 'I have to, Tamara. I don't see how you can possibly love me after the way I treated you over Anna. How can you ever forgive me for that, Tamara? How?'

Tamara could have wept at the pain in his eyes. 'There's nothing to forgive, Kiel. I understand. I'd have probably felt the same if the positions were reversed.'

'You're one in a million.' His arms tightened around her, his mouth found hers, and it was bliss being able to return his kiss without worrying that she was giving herself away. A glorious joy soared through her.

'You mean everything to me, do you know that?' he breathed, his eyes deep and dark with desire, a fingertip reverently tracing the outline of her face. 'You are my night and my day, you are the sun that warms me and the love that feeds me.' Another kiss and a lifetime later he stopped to draw breath.

'I wish my father were alive to see us now,' she said softly.

Kiel nodded. 'I think the only reason he left me the company was so that we would be forced into each other's company. He never knew that I blamed you for Anna's death.'

'And I resented you because you'd got what I wanted most.'

He grinned ruefully. 'It wasn't a very good basis for a working relationship, was it? Or any other sort of relationship? It must have cost you a lot, Tamara, to engineer this meeting.'

'A lifetime's pride,' she admitted. 'And I thought I'd failed.'

'Oh, lord, Tamara.' He groaned anew. 'I've treated you despicably. Especially that night in London. If only I'd known then that you loved me. I took your most precious possession and immediately hated myself for it. Not many girls your age are still virgins. I thought you were saving yourself for the right man.'

'I was.' She smiled. 'You.'

'I still think I did the wrong thing in making love to you, but I loved you so much that my judgement was distorted. Oh, lord, have I suffered because of that night.'

'Please, Kiel, don't blame yourself any longer. We've both suffered in our own ways, but I think we should now put everything behind us and start a new life right from this very moment.'

'How can you be so forgiving?'

She smiled, the soft, gentle smile of a woman in love. 'Because I love you, Kiel. I think I always have, ever since that time you kissed me when I was eighteen. I've tried to fight it, believe me I've tried.'

He drew in a deep, agonised breath. 'I think the truth of the matter is that I was half in love with you as well, which made it all the harder after the accident. I couldn't love a girl who'd killed my sister—that's what I told myself, that's why I was so hard on you. I still can't believe my good fortune. I want to marry you straight away, Tamara, before you change your mind.'

She smiled serenely. 'I'd marry you this minute, Kiel, if it were possible.'

He kissed her again, and when they eventually and reluctantly drew apart she said, 'I think I'll ring my mother. This is all her doing. She knew I loved you and she's as bad as my father for wanting to see the two of us married.'

'I loved Ben, Tamara.'

'I know. He'd be so happy if he were here now.'

'I'm sure he's looking down on us.'

'Will you come back and take over, Kiel?'

He nodded.

'It will be a family company once again,' she said with satisfaction.

'You won't resent me running it? You won't question my decisions?'

She grinned impishly. 'Not if I agree with them. But I'm sure you wouldn't want a meek and mild little wife?'

'Tamara, I don't think you could ever be that. Your fighting spirit is part of your charm. The day you found out I'd taken over the company you stormed into my office like a bat out of hell—and life hasn't been the same since.'

She grinned, tracing her finger over his lips. 'You can tell your friend that I won't be needing his flat after all, because I'm moving in with you. In fact I think I might move in tonight and see if I can disrupt your life even further.'

He covered her face with tiny kisses. 'I can't think of anything I'd like more.'

HARLEQUIN PROUDLY PRESENTS A DAZZLING CONCEPT IN ROMANCE FICTION

One small town,
twelve terrific love stories.

TYLER—GREAT READING... GREAT SAVINGS... AND A FABULOUS FREE GIFT

Each book set in Tyler is a self-contained love story;
together, the twelve novels stitch the fabric of
the community.

By collecting proofs-of-purchase found in each Tyler
book, you can receive a fabulous gift, ABSOLUTELY
FREE! And use our special Tyler coupons to save on
your next Tyler book purchase.

Join us for the third Tyler book, WISCONSIN
WEDDING by Carla Neggers, available in May.

Following the success of WITH THIS RING, Harlequin cordially invites you to enjoy the romance of the wedding season with

BARBARA BRETTON
RITA CLAY ESTRADA
SANDRA JAMES
DEBBIE MACOMBER

A collection of romantic stories that celebrate the joy, excitement, and mishaps of planning that special day by these four award-winning Harlequin authors.

Available in April at your favorite Harlequin retail outlets.

⬧ Harlequin ®

JANELLE TAYLOR

Valley of Fire

HARLEQUIN IS PROUD TO PRESENT *VALLEY OF FIRE* BY JANELLE TAYLOR—AUTHOR OF TWENTY-TWO BOOKS, INCLUDING SIX *NEW YORK TIMES* BESTSELLERS

VALLEY OF FIRE—the warm and passionate story of Kathy Alexander, a famous romance author, and Steven Winngate, entrepreneur and owner of the magazine that intended to expose the real Kathy "Brandy" Alexander to her fans.

Don't miss VALLEY OF FIRE, available in May.